# THE TALES OF TIME

Made in the USA
Columbia, SC
21 September 2024

42095014R00076

# THE TALES OF TIME

L. MARIE WOOD

FALSTAFF
BOOKS
WWW.FALSTAFFBOOKS.COM

# PENNY CANDY

PENNY CANDY loosely wrapped in dirty parchment paper. Lined up on a counter so caked with grime I could write my name in it. I did write my name in it after all, feeling like I had to, like it was the last thing I would ever do.

Stuckey wuz here.

I sighed as I looked at the parchment paper covering something that didn't look like candy at all. Too big. Too long. Too lumpy to be peanut brittle like the man said it was. The man who was sweating and breathing heavy as he looked at me. The man whose fingers twitched as I watched. The day's special, he said, when I came into the store looking for some sunflower seeds. Try it, you'll like it. Something about the way he looked at me, about the way the door clicked when it closed, like it was locking me in, something about the haze in the dingy old everything store made me think I'd better try it if I knew what was good for me.

Penny candy loosely wrapped in dirty parchment paper. Waiting for me. Mine to eat. As much as I wanted. But I knew as my dry tongue tried to retreat down my throat, I would only be able to stomach one.

# $5.99

THE MOVIE WENT OFF and cycled back to the main screen, burning the stationary main page into the plasma TV more and more with every passing second. Carla had fallen asleep in front of the television again, as she had most nights since she got the DVD, unable to pull herself away from the screen to make it to bed. That really wasn't true though. She hadn't made it to bed because she didn't want to go to bed. She was right where she wanted to be.

Her sister thought she was crazy. Not literally, but she would have if she knew—if she *believed*. It wasn't like Carla hadn't tried to tell her, hadn't tried to share him with her... once... in the beginning. But Carla's sister didn't see it. He didn't speak to Tami the way he spoke to Carla. It was only right, really. He was Carla's, after all.

There wasn't anything special about the DVD, just a B-level movie with a cast that you think you might have seen before, but if so, you can't remember where. Carla got it out of one of those bins full of surplus movies discounted to $5.99.

But that wasn't all it was. Not to Carla.

The storyline was slow-paced and didn't really go anywhere, but Carla wasn't listening to the lines. The actors either never really "made it," were over-the-hill has-beens, or were newbies, but Carla recognized one of them. She should. She had seen him in her dreams for years.

Well, not him specifically, and not in the dreams like the ones you have when you're sleeping. But in her fantasies, in her daydreams, he was always there. He looked like a combination of her first love, a guy she knew from work, and the last guy she slept with. Such an odd mix, with unkempt hair, deep, penetrating eyes, the most sensuous lips. Carla could hardly tear her eyes away from the screen when he was in a scene and found herself reaching for the remote to fast-forward to his next one even if it meant she'd have no idea what was going on in the movie when she got there.

After her second time watching the movie all the way through, he started talking to her.

At first it was just a look. He would look at the screen, seemingly at her, when he should have been looking at the actor opposite him. The first look was just a peek, just a glance; Carla almost didn't notice it at all. His second look was so much more meaningful. There was a playful twist to his lips that was endearing. His third look was downright obscene, the way he licked those luscious lips of his and lowered his eyelids. It gave Carla chills. The good kind.

Twenty minutes into the movie he spoke to her.

"Carla."

She felt as though she was waking from a dream when she heard her name. He was looking at her again, full on, shoulders squared to the screen—watching her. He was smiling just enough for her to see a hint of white from his teeth. She felt herself respond though she knew she shouldn't. He didn't have many lines in the movie; he was nothing more than a glorified extra, really, yet he had spoken her name as clearly as if he were sitting in the room whispering it in her ear. Carla spun her head around, looking in all corners of the room to be sure that he—that someone—wasn't there making fun of her, laughing at her expense. But she was alone.

With him.

She watched the movie three more times that day and more that weekend, blowing off shopping with her sister, a date with a guy she had been interested in for months, sleeping in her bed, and eating. With every viewing he said more to her, sometimes telling her how beautiful she was, pouting his lips as he spoke, letting her see all the curves and contortions they went through as they formed words, other times asking her to remove garments so he could see more. She felt silly and excited at the same time. It was weird, strange; all of those things, but it was the best fantasy she'd ever had.

As Carla snored, catching her first reluctant winks in 30 hours, the screen flickered and blinked before finally catching again on the beginning of the movie. For a second, gone faster than Carla's eyes could have deciphered had she been awake, a roiling sea of red bubbled to the surface, washing Carla's face in blood as a tentacle reached out to stroke her cheek.

# INHERITANCE

To Wilson's credit, his attempt had been a good one. Sharon was surprised he'd had the presence of mind and initiative to call Hattie into service before Sharon could find a suitable slave. The argument must have really burned him up, so much he went straight home that night and set to the business of concocting his potion. But Hattie had been easy to dissuade, at least thus far. Sharon didn't have to do much more than lock the door against her to keep her at bay. A quick sidestep and the old girl was lost. Wilson hadn't bothered to teach Hattie anything more than how to get up and walk again. He told her to go after Sharon and to kill her, but he hadn't told her how.

Sharon got used to the beating against her front door. Hattie could stay out there all night if she wanted to. It didn't bother Sharon any, and there wasn't a neighbor to complain about the noise for miles. She figured Wilson would wait until morning to see if Hattie had done the job. At least until after the funeral, just so it would look right. People would wonder why he wasn't in the family car, it being his brother-in-law's funeral and all. They would wonder why he would be anywhere except right by his wife's side.

Sharon had time.

Hattie hadn't figured out that she would do better to bust in the windows yet. Sharon doubted that she would. The woman hadn't been a brain surgeon in life. How could she be expected to do better in death? Sharon sucked her teeth as she walked into the spare bathroom, the room where she brewed her potions and cast her spells. She thought back on how they had gotten to the place they were now—wanting to rip each other limb from limb as soon as look at one another.

Their mother had left the shop to both of them. She had been a respected woman in their village, a woman who was known to take care of people's problems. Half the time she didn't do anything except sell roots and dried fruit for one potion or the next; she told Sharon and Wilson herself that the whole thing was bogus. But it worked, and she never had to put in a hard day's labor in the hot sun in her life.

Wilson played around with it; 'Momma's mumbo-jumbo,' he called it. He was the oldest and the one who was supposed to inherit the business. He never caught on though, and was easily overshadowed by his younger sister, who seemed to have the real gift. When their mother died, she left everything to the both of them. And that's where the trouble started.

"You're making us look like fools," Sharon said from the back room of the shop that day. "No one will believe us if you keep gallivanting around the street like a commoner."

"They don't believe us as it is, Sharon," he said, tired of the argument. It was always the same thing over and over. "People are smarter now. They know this is a bunch of bullshit."

Sharon burst through the beads that hung from the

ceiling to separate the rooms and growled, "Watch your tongue in momma's house."

Wilson chuckled. "Sharon, momma's been dead for ten years already. When are you gonna cut it out?" He turned his back to his sister and touched one of the dry herbs that hung from the ceiling.

"Her *ánimo* is still here, Wilson. She's angry that you speak of her that way."

"Right, sure," he said condescendingly. "Anyhow, I just came here to tell you that I'll be talking with a man about selling this dump. I'm gonna try and get whatever money we can out of this place and do something with it. Maybe I'll move to the mainland. Who knows?"

Sharon looked stricken. "You can't sell the place! This is momma's legacy!"

Wilson flicked the herb and sent it swinging on the string that held it. "It's not much of a legacy, now is it? We can barely live on what we make from it. I have to work a second job just to keep food on the table." He shook his head and stood to leave. "I'm selling it, Sharon. And there's nothing you can do about it."

Wilson walked toward the door, opened it, and turned to speak before leaving. "But you should have already known that, *bruha*."

Sharon cursed him then, vowing to stop him by any means necessary. She didn't utter a sound as she stood facing the closed door of her mother's shop, but Wilson heard every word.

\* \* \*

THE CHURCH WAS STICKY, and the mosquitoes relentless. They couldn't resist the bounty they were getting: thirty people

7

crammed in a small church with nothing but their hands to protect them. They feasted.

Wilson escorted his wife in and sat in front of the body of her brother. Clay had been a strong man, muscular and fit for most of his life, but that didn't save him. He worked out on the boats and was stung by a Portuguese Man of War during an afternoon pull. They didn't make it back to the dock in time to save him after he went into cardiac arrest.

As his wife sobbed, all Wilson could think about was Sharon. She wasn't at the funeral, so she must be dead. She wouldn't have missed Clay's service. She fancied him and was genuinely saddened by his death. Wilson tried to conceal his smile as he thought of Hattie taking Sharon by surprise. She must have been shocked to see her, considering she had attended Hattie's funeral a couple of days earlier. He would talk to the man after they put Clay in the ground, Wilson surmised. He would have his money in less than a month.

His wife's shaking grew intense, and a cry was stuck in her throat, choking her. Wilson turned to her and said, "Honey? Honey, are you ok?" He didn't see Clay fidgeting in his tight casket, didn't recognize the sounds of grunting from his chest and the ripping of the stitches in his lips to be what they were. His wife's eyes were wide open, unblinking, in shock. "Honey?" He shook her slightly, trying to get her attention and pull her out of day terror she was having. She wouldn't look at him.

Wilson turned his head in the direction of his wife's stare in time to see Clay sit up in the casket. An audible moan escaped his chest as the air escaped his lungs. Clay forced his mouth and eyes open, ripping the stitches apart. He lifted his right arm and then his left, inspecting them in disbelief. The whole thing was so much déjà vu to Wilson that he didn't move.

Then Clay climbed out of the casket.

Wilson didn't hear the shrieks and screams that emanated from the congregation as Clay planted his feet on the floor. He only saw Sharon standing at the back of the church smiling prettily, devilishly.

Clay moved quickly for one of the undead. He closed the space between himself and Wilson in three strides and pressed down on his shoulders, buckling his legs, making him submit. Wilson became aware of a pungent odor, the smell of meat that had been left out in the sun. Sharon had converted Hattie in the light of day and brought her along as backup.

With everything he could remember from Momma, with everything he had, he called Hattie inside. She came sluggishly, bewildered. She looked at Sharon who was too busy watching the show in front of her to notice. Then she looked at Wilson.

He intimated his command to her, deftly breaking Sharon's spell and reinforcing his own. Hattie was upon Sharon before she could turn around. He wished she had; Wilson would have loved to have seen the look of surprised terror on Sharon's face.

*I'm better than you now, sister. I bloomed right under your nose.*

The smell of fresh blood permeated the air as Hattie ripped away Sharon's scalp. Sharon's scream was nothing more than an afterthought as was her limp hand against Hattie's decaying cheek. She was dead as soon as her skull was exposed to the summer air. Hattie banged Sharon's head against the wall like a squirrel might a nut and pawed at the brain inside.

Clay smelled the blood just before Wilson did. He turned his head, loosening his grip just enough for Wilson to slip away. Clay lunged at Sharon, grabbing her leg and digging his nails into her skin, cutting through the flesh and muscle with determined swipes. He licked at the blood that spewed from the wounds before baring his teeth and biting into the supple flesh. Wilson slinked against the wall, trying to make a quiet exit while Hattie and Clay dined on Sharon. He noticed for the first time that the church was empty; everyone had fled, running for their lives, including his wife. He'd have to remember that she hadn't tried to help him at all, that she had just left him in there to deal with two zombies. Yes, that was useful information indeed.

Wilson stood in the doorway to watch as Clay sank his teeth into Sharon for another bite, sinews and fatty tissue draped over his working lips. He looked at Sharon's face one last time, at her ruined eyes and what was left of her exposed brain and smiled. As he closed the door to the church, his expression transformed from grim satisfaction to abject fear to please the waiting crowd. His wife ran up to him, tears streaming from her eyes, wetting her cheeks. He hugged her hurriedly, burying his face in her welcoming neck, deftly hiding the hatred in his eyes.

He'd meet the man later that day. He'd have his money in less than a month.

# CEMETERY ROAD

I'VE NEVER BEEN afraid of the dark, but I'm damned scared now. Donnie said the trees looked like legs in the dark, and he was right. My flashlight ain't helpin' things either, just makes 'em look like they're moving.

I don't know why I'm here, but I am.

I know'd better than to come up here, but I dint use the sense God gave me. They was just talking so much shit about how I wasn't gonna do it and how I was a chicken shit, that I just had to. So I'm here, and I wish I wasn't.

I drove up to the corner, like they said to, and parked the car. They said they'd be watching to see if I would do it, so I followed every instruction. I dint want them to say I cheated. And I damned sure don't want to do it again. I started walking up the road and zipped up my jacket. It was cold as hell outside, no kind of weather to go playing around in a cemetery, but then again, when was? My footsteps sounded loud as I walked up the deserted road, not a car to be seen. I started to count the crunching of the rocks—made the time go by quicker. By the time I got to 150, I had made it up the hill and could see the headstones shining off my flashlight. The white ones seemed to glow.

Houses lined the street, every one of them with dark windows. Who the hell would want to live across the street from a cemetery anyway? Even if it doesn't spook you, it ain't nothing to look at. The only people ever outside are crying.

Six, maybe seven houses stood there and nobody in any of 'em. For some reason that don't set right with me.

I looked at the tombstones, trying to decide if I was going in or not. My granddaddy's stone was on the edge of the street, damned near paved over when they put up the new road back in '84. It leaned to the side, sunken in the ground, chunks taken out of it from the wind and rain. Just beat up. *That's what's gonna happen to me*, I thought as I stared at it sticking out of the ground like a broken tooth. Something about that made me want to run.

I looked back at the houses with their black eyes staring at me. I couldn't tell which one I felt safer having my back to. The cold made me decide quick.

I looked back to the cemetery and saw the same tombstones, the same trees, and decided to go in. Ain't no difference in a cemetery in the day or at night. Dead people there all the time, and they can't bother nobody. And anyway, Donnie and the guys're watchin'.

The first step inside was hard, but they got easier after that. I walked past granddaddy's grave and on down the Barlow line, ending up by my cousin who just got put in the ground a couple months back. I snickered at his grave and thought for a second about leaving that $5.00 I owed him on the grass, but nah. Why waste good money on someone who can't use it anymore? Poor sucker.

This shit is easy once you get the balls to do it. I walked around like I owned the place. Thought about what it might cost to buy a place like this. Make money off putting people in the ground? You could stack three or four coffins on top of each other and charge for a single plot! Do that over so many acres and you got a goldmine. Might need to look into it tomorrow when I get up.

I figured that was enough after I got to Sandy Laurelton's grave. Old biddy died back in 1837 at the age of, what was it, 96? I think that's what the cross said, but it was pretty splintered, so I could be wrong. Either way, old is old. I gave the back of Sandy's cross a slap like she'd probably never had on her ass when she was alive and started back the way I came, happy this shit is over. I dare them to talk shit about me now.

When I saw them coming I couldn't help but call out. And why did it matter anyway? Dead people don't care how loud you are.

"Hey Donnie!" I yelled, steam filling up the air like a white cloud. "I did it, dude! Smacked this little bitch on the ass too."

I thought Donnie would get a kick out of that. Hell, he's the one who likes to fuck 'em when they're damned near dead anyway. But he dint say anything. Well fuck him then, the jealous little bitch. I probably stayed in longer than him, and he was pissed. So who's the chicken shit now?

I stopped walking and let them get closer, the cloud in front of my face going in and out as I caught my breath. They dint have a cloud in front of theirs.

# IDOL

"How can he be that beautiful?"

Millie stared in awe at the image on her smartphone, enlarging his lips, his eyes, even his undercut for a closer look. The sigh that escaped her lips was heavy with sweet admiration and laced with feels she hadn't been aware of before finding K-Pop. It didn't take long for her to become entrenched in the mania. She found her favorite group almost right away, their luxurious voices caressing lyrics she didn't understand, creating an exotic, taboo-like aura in her room when she put on their songs... which was every day, for most of the day. She bought all the stuff: the summer video packages, the CDs with special photo albums inside, the swag featuring her bias and the one showcasing her bias wrecker (then, guiltily, something with the faces of the other members too because how could she truly be a fan if she only supported a few of the members, right?). Millie had it all. They were going to be performing in the US later that year, and Millie had a great idea to pitch to her mom about travelling to LA to see them. LA is a lot closer than South Korea, she would say. I can work during the summer to help out on costs, she would add. Maybe her mom would understand. She'd had her own entertainer crush, right? I mean, what were all those tears about when Prince died if she didn't? Millie thought she probably shouldn't go there, not unless she really had to. Mom hadn't listened to Prince since he died – the mourning was real.

His oval eyes looked out at her from behind a fan of periwinkle-colored bangs (oh, how her bias loved to change his hair color!), giving all the fanservice he knew she and the millions of other screaming teenage girls around the world liked. He had just woken up in some other place on the other side of the world from where she sat and decided to go live on YouTube just because. Millie grinned from ear to ear when she got the notification and left the dinner table without warning. Her father said, "Don't forget about the movie," or something like that as she passed by him. Millie had shoved earbuds in her ears before taking her plate to the sink and had turned the volume up high so that she could hear every nuance of his voice before reaching the stairs.

She thought she grunted a response to her father but wasn't sure.

His face was filling her screen before she had gotten out of the room; his perfect pink lips parted suggestively as he worked to get the camera situated just right. She never saw her brother Chris smirking at her from the kitchen as she raced by, never saw her cat dodging her legs as they scissored wildly up the stairs. She only saw him, only heard his groggy voice speaking in his hypnotic foreign tongue.

He yawned.
Millie smiled.
He chuckled.
Millie blushed.

\* \* \*

"MILLIE HASN'T COME DOWN YET?" her mother asked of no one in particular. The kitchen was clean, and the leftovers put away. It was time for movie night, and three of the four of their little family were ready to get started.

Chris looked up, shrugged, and turned his attention back to the game he was playing on his smartphone. Millie's father sighed and said, "No, not yet."

Millie's mom looked up at the ceiling, a move she swore helped her to hear what was going on upstairs better, and listened intently. The muffled sound of a male voice speaking quickly could be heard. She didn't notice the staticky hiss that was deliberately, persistently there, but inconspicuously so. Like the assumption of crackling on the wind after an electric shock, the sound floated among the waves and pitch to mingle with his rich baritone. She strained, trying to understand something of what was being said, trying to determine whether the broadcast was almost over or not. She wanted to give her daughter a chance to join the family activity on her own. Choosing her battles these days, Millie's mom didn't relish the idea of pulling her away from something she wanted to do. On any given day, Millie might as easily bite her head off as give her a smile, and if the guy that was talking was the one from that K-Pop group she liked, and Millie tried to interrupt her...

"Go get your sister," their mom said to Chris reluctantly.

Chris' nose was stuck in the game. He was oblivious.

She looked at Chris and then over at her husband incredulously.

He cleared his throat first but got no reaction.

"Chris!" His voice boomed in the room.

Chris looked up, surprised.

"Your mother told you to go and get your sister."

The protest that rose in Chris' throat died on his lips when he saw the frustration in his father's eyes. He got up without a word, leaving his phone behind as he knew they wanted him to. Chris didn't want to fight. He wanted to watch the movie. This week had been his choice and he couldn't wait to rub it in Millie's face. He had chosen *Child's Play*, mostly because he knew Millie hated Chuckie. Crazy little demon doll, here we come.

Chris bounded up the stairs, talking all the way. "Time to say goodnight, sweetheart," he parodied, trying to sound lovey-dovey. "It's time for the movie." He stopped outside her door, hearing a male voice speaking in a language he didn't understand. "You don't even know what he's saying, Mil." Chris turned the knob and opened her door, still talking. "He could be telling you to take off your clothes in front of class and do the dance from his last video." This struck Chris as incredibly funny.

Chris' hearty laughter turned shrill, like the scream of a siren, when his sister turned toward him slowly. It wasn't the saliva that spilled from the corners of her mouth that frightened him most, nor the milky white veil that covered her chestnut brown irises. It was the way she spoke that sent chills down his spine; the monotone delivery of a question he could not understand,

"Eotteohge geuleohge aleumdab ji?"

# NEW HOUSE

I CAN SEE them from my window.

Some glisten in the moonlight, others cast shadows along the darkened path—the one that leads to our place. The tallest of them all acts like a sentinel, watching over the rest as they reach toward the sky unabashedly. Do they call to the others to reach out too, the ones who hesitate, beckoning them to break free and stretch out their hands?

I can hear them.

Disturbing the ground, roots snapping, dead grass crunching, earth shifting to fall inside... earth smudging the satiny white pillow. I hear them.

I hear them grunt and wheeze and whistle with effort as the wind whips around them, courses through them, pushes, and pulls.

Silence floods my ears like a freshet; loud, empty, ripping, still.

Gargling, gnashing, grunting as my house creaks, groans, and burbles in the settling.

Warped shadows on the path limping to, fro, away, toward, as the moon sits high and the clouds pass low.

Tall trees, fern leaves, evergreen, limp hair.

Cloth centuries old ripped from bindings left to float in the wind, twisting, turning, writhing as they disintegrate into dust.

The dust from which they came.

Ashes to ashes.

New house trash littering the lawn.

Packing peanuts fill the new hole.

# FAMILY DINNER

"YOU GOTTA BE KIDDING ME," Nick said as he turned onto the dark road... a road that looked just like the last one, and the one before. He had been driving for an hour into the deep woods and across state lines for a girl he had just met. *Come to dinner* she had whispered in his ear the week before. *Meet my family.*

Already?

They had only been out on a few dates, had only spent maybe 7 hours together, but who's counting? She talked about cavern hunting (who can resist stalactites and stalagmites?) and great skiing when he got there, but that wasn't the reason he said yes. It was her. She wore such a sweet smile when she asked him to come, looked so perfect in her tight jeans and loose sweater. She felt so warm when he hugged her close and felt her form underneath all that knit, so he said sure. It didn't matter that her family dinner was the same day that he was celebrating a win with his buddies, sending him in the other direction from her folks' house and adding 45 minutes to an already long drive.

Amy.

All that mattered was the smile she would greet him with when she opened the door and the warm hug that waited for him.

Assuming he could ever get there.

The drive from Fairfax was the easy part. He knew his old stomping grounds well enough to make it most of the way out of Northern Virginia and over to Warrenton, where the city lights were a distant memory, but that was as far as he could go without help. It didn't help that there was no interstate to get onto. The closest one would have put him a half hour out of his way, so he braved the side streets and back roads, relying on his GPS and, after a while, instinct. GPS, God love it. Such a great tool when it works. But like that early-adopt model he won at a casino in the late 90s, the one that had to be suction-cupped to his windshield and that sent him into the Baltimore harbor every time he made a turn off Pratt Street, the route his phone gave him was no use. It kept rerouting as if the mountains surrounding the sleepy hamlet grew up overnight, making a once-usable road impassible. Nick had gotten so sick of hearing that unaccented, mild-mannered female voice telling him to make a U-turn, he closed the app.

White's Taxidermy on his left. Margie's Good Eats on the right. Coincidence?

Nick would have laughed at his joke if he hadn't already told it before. He was sure he passed a similar combination a few towns back. Taxidermist Tull and Jake's Steak. Forever Pets Taxidermy and The Rib Shack. It was funny the first time, but not anymore.

Nick pulled into a gas station. He was happy to find one of those big chain stations like the ones he was used to at home. The drive itself was starting to look like one of those low-budget horror movies—he didn't need to add a broken down, one-pump station with the stereotypically grimy gas jockey to the mix. He and three other people filed into the brightly-lit convenience store at the station. He listened as the person in front of him asked for directions to the ski lodge near where Amy's family lived—the same one that had a hot chocolate with his name on it waiting by a warm fire. The route sounded like the one he had just come off, long and twisty and dark. When it was his turn, Nick told the attendant—young and clean, thank you very much—that he was looking for directions to the same place.

"But where's the highway," Nick asked after being given the same directions the woman before him got. "There's gotta be something that cuts through these mountains instead of sticking to the back roads." He picked up a candy bar and laid it on the counter. "I feel like I've been driving around forever."

The young man nodded imperceptibly, his eye twitching under the patch of highlighted hair visible beneath the rim of his red service cap. "I wish, but there's nothing like that," he said a little too eagerly. "This is the best way to get out to the ski lodge, especially since it's almost dark."

Nick smiled at him incredulously. That's why he wanted the highway! The afternoon light was fading fast, and he did not relish the idea of driving around the woods on winding roads in the dark. He did not want hitting a deer to be in his future.

"There's gotta be something. I mean, there's no way trucks take these narrow streets to deliver to you. What do they use?"

The attendant rang up his candy bar without looking at him.

Nick tried again. "I saw lights, but I couldn't get to them."

Giving Nick his change, the attendant said, "I don't know. But the directions I gave you will get you to the ski lodge in about 2 hours."

The attendant held out his bag with hands that looked like they could be shaking. Just a little, but it was there. Nick shook his head, thanked him, and got back in the car. Two hours? He'd been driving for an hour already, and the GPS said it was just about 2 hours away from where he started. Could he really be that far off course?

Nick looked in the direction that the attendant told him to go. Two of the three cars that came in with him headed that way. The other car, a guy in a button-down shirt open at the neck and dress slacks driving a non-descript black sedan that screamed company car, went the other way. Nick climbed into his own car and turned it on fast. He could feel the attendant's eyes on him, beseeching him to go the way he had been told, but Nick ignored the sensation as it crept up his back to caress his neck. He followed the company car even as the gas station attendant screamed, "No!"

Leafless trees.

Asphalt.

Dead grass.

Repeat.

There was nothing. Not even a boarded-up house to break up the monotony. Nothing at all. Nick had caught up with the other rebel and was right behind him. The man had even made a saluting gesture to him in his rearview mirror—just two compadres bucking the system. It was getting late. At 4:30, it was almost completely dark. There were no street-lights on the country road, but Nick could see some off in the distance. The road traversed a lazy hill. If he could just get down to those lights, Nick was sure he'd find a way that would cut through the spiderweb of back roads and take him where he needed to be. Amy's family lived in a college town—there were bound to be major routes leading to it. He just needed to find one.

Oh crap, Amy!

She had to be worried. Nick picked up his phone and noticed she had called twice already. When? He had the phone with him when he was in the gas station, and it had been sitting in the cupholder the whole time he was driving. It never rang.

"Technology," Nick said out loud, "Gotta love it."

Nick dialed Amy's number and heard nothing. No ringing, no beeping, no 'all circuits are busy' message—nothing.

He looked at his phone, taking his eyes away from the road for a second to see if he had missed a number somehow. He had just added her number to his favorites list, but now he wondered if he had put the number in wrong. Nick didn't see the front end of the company car disappear like it got sucked through an invisible portal. The man threw the car in reverse, and it lurched backwards. The doors seemed to stretch, pulling away from the side panels as if running from a magnet. The metal pulled like saltwater taffy, stretching in long lines of silver and black. The back tires spun against the asphalt, digging for purchase but finding none.

Nick didn't hear the tires screeching on the road, nor the muted screams left behind like an echo as the man travelled through the barrier. He didn't notice the country road rippling as it engulfed the non-descript sedan, the facade rising and falling like paper in the wind to reveal a glimpse of a black core that seemed to pulse with life. He never saw how flat the landscape was, how it mirrored itself every few yards, like cheap floor tiles keeping pattern. Instead, he heard the unaccented, mild-mannered female voice of his GPS telling him to turn around to start route guidance, only this time she was screaming.

# THE EVER AFTER

# CHAPTER ONE

Oh my God.

I couldn't stop myself from screaming. I had been screaming since it started. I breathed in and out, in and out, only vaguely registering the odd taste of the air, the sulfuric smell.

Dead.

I must be dead. Surely after a fall from so high, no one could have survived. I looked around at the bodies that littered the field, legs askance, arms bent at impossible angles, and I nodded. We're all dead.

My eyes watered as I looked up at the brilliant blue sky. I was up there. A shiver ran through me as I remembered. It was midday, maybe two or three o'clock—exactly the time when I always start to feel restless at my desk. I wanted the day to be over. I wanted to go out in the sunshine and play. Sometimes I wondered if I was really cut out to work in an office. The walls seemed to close in on me. I couldn't focus, didn't want to think. I hated my cube walls. I hated my officemates. I hated the work. So uninteresting. So unimportant. I wanted to do something real, something that mattered.

I was on the way outside for my normal break (I took five every day even though I don't smoke), and I was itching to get outside. I passed people I knew in the hall and mumbled hello, shared the elevator with someone and engaged in the obligatory chitchat, then barely stopped myself from running out of the front door.

"Enjoy your break."

That's what he said. Enjoy your break. Such a normal comment, a throwaway, something you really don't mean but you say just to be nice. It's like when people say, 'Have a good day!' or 'How are you?' They don't really want a response; they don't want to listen to some long, drawn out story. They just needed something to say. *Enjoy your break*. If he hadn't said it I would have escaped the image of what he would become.

"Enjoy your break," said the guard whose name I never knew. His smile was genuine enough, but he wasn't even looking at me when he said it. He had already moved on to the next person, addressing someone else from his cramped little room. I was just another faceless person to speak to as they passed in and out of the lobby. I smiled back anyway, a thin-lipped thing that could just as easily have been a grimace. And that's when it happened.

Gravity gave way.

First my hair lifted off my head and rose above me like a crown, then my feet lifted off the ground. What I felt was confirmed by what I saw: the guard, several inches taller than me, rose off the ground and struck the low ceiling of his security shack before he could even scream. Instead of stopping, he pressed through, breaking into the ceiling. There was a horrible sound—a wet, cracking, popping noise. Blood, bone, and matter rained down in a torrent from the hole he created.

Oh my God.

In one wild instant I caught a glimpse of the world below me. My purse had fallen off my shoulder and was lying on the ground. Papers and pencils littered the guard's desk to be splattered with his blood. None of those things were floating up to oblivion. This wasn't gravity giving way. This was something else.

I screamed for the guard as much as for myself. It was only after hearing my own voice that I realized I was moving toward the higher ceiling of the lobby and toward that poor man's same fate. I grabbed the doorframe and pulled myself outside, ducking through with barely enough time to clear the rest of my body before colliding with the doorframe. For the briefest of moments I tried to will my feet down to the ground, but there was no chance. It was as if I was on an invisible lift being raised up. My ascent was beyond my control.

People outside rose with me, some above me, some below me, some in sync with me. The ascent wasn't quick, and that was the torture of it; the ride was slow enough for me to take in what was happening, just long enough for me to become afraid. Smoke from car accidents below billowed up to us, giving chase. There was so much screaming and crying. Some cursing. Lots of praying. People tried to move toward each other craving touch, a hand to hold as we rose to our deaths. Surely that's what we were doing—rising to our deaths. Soon we wouldn't be able to breathe, or we'd freeze to death or…

I laughed through my tears. Leave it to me to forget which would happen first. Jenny the airhead forever. Never taking anything seriously. But this was serious all right. It was the end of the world.

Windows broke, and people rose through them, bloodied. Glass protruded out of open wounds, heads cut open to reveal the smooth sheen of bone. Severed heads and detached limbs rose from the crashes below, bobbing on the wind like grotesque Macy's parade float inflatables.

Babies cried. Perhaps that was the worst part.

The air started to get cold, and I began to understand with unwanted clarity that it wouldn't be long now. If gravity kicked in at this point, the drop would crush me. If I didn't stop rising, I would freeze to death. If I escaped that death somehow, I would not be able to breathe outside of Earth's atmosphere. That's the order, I realized after all. Crazily I wondered if a spaceship would pick me up. Would I stop on a cloud and see my grandmother waiting there? Delirium had already begun to set in.

My life had been aimless, a collection of unfulfilled dreams and wishful thinking. And now it was over. I cried for myself—for what I wanted to do but hadn't, for the pain I would surely feel when I met my end regardless of how. I shut my eyes to the terrifying world before me and opened them to this one with the strange blue sky above my head and rough grass beneath me. People lay scattered on the ground, lifeless, except the ones who sat ramrod straight looking up at the sun with unblinking, inky eyes.

When I sat up under that freakishly blue sky, they all turned to look at me.

# CHAPTER TWO

*I WASN'T GOING to cut her.*

The thought greeted me as I woke up in the comically green crabgrass. Even as it flitted away out of my grasp, I knew it was a lie. I meant to cut her and had wanted to from the moment I knew I was ready to leave. I just didn't have the guts to do it.

*But I did it, didn't I?*

I saw the knife in my hand, saw myself raising it above my head and thrusting it down fast. I heard Felicia yelling at me in that condescending way until she felt the blade pierce her skin. Then she screamed in pain. And fear.

I remember liking that part most of all.

I remember telling her that I couldn't take it anymore, that she needed to act like a woman and not a man. I already have a man, and he knew his role. She needed to learn hers. But she wouldn't. When I wanted her, it was because I craved soft, sexy, alluring—pretty, damn it. Not bossy, foul-mouthed, and rough.

She wasn't always that way. When we started seeing each other, she was sweet and loving. Her face lit up when she saw me. She used to call me Brandy when I hit it right. But when I met Paul and brought him home—when I kissed Paul before kissing her—she changed. She was waiting; I knew that. She was waiting for me to choose her over Paul. She pretended to like our three-way romance and probably did enjoy the sex if she didn't think about it too much. But she wanted me for herself, and not having me made her mad and mean.

Cutting her meant I had chosen. Finally.

My apartment was covered in blood. The walls were splashed with it as I chased her around. Once I started cutting I had to finish, but she wouldn't stay still. I was on top of her when it happened, making sure she was dead. Her body was warm between my legs. Her little titties were pushed together in her bra, teasing me for the last time.

*I should have fucked her one more time before I killed her.*

I was thinking that when the sky fell.

It seemed like a cutaway for a TV show; my vision went all white for a second and then gradually came back, showing me this new, weird world. What I saw when I opened my eyes didn't make sense. People were staggering, leaning, falling over. I saw bodies on the ground—some were moving, but others were still. Most people were just staring up at that crazy sky. I looked too. I felt like I was being hypnotized. My body rocked, moving like a dandelion in the breeze. I imagined that my head was like the white fuzz on a dandelion with seeds blowing off in the wind. My hair, nose, and ears blew off too, twisting and turning in the wind and leaving droplets of blood on the ground.

That image is what snapped me out of it—whatever 'it' was.

I looked down, certain I would see Felicia beneath me, her chest destroyed by that piece of shit knife I used on her. I was covered in blood, had to be; I could almost feel it coating my arms. But there wasn't any blood at all. No knife either. And Felicia was nowhere to be found.

I was kneeling in grass with thick, curly lime-greenish blades that seemed to creep toward me in the wind, like they wanted to wrap around my ankles. I shook my head and laughed at myself as I stood up, only distantly wondering where these crazy thoughts were coming from. I felt a lot of things in that moment but the main thing was relief. And power.

I felt fucking awesome.

I killed my lady ('that bitch' seemed too harsh a name for her now) and got away with it. It was all cleaned up and left behind. It didn't matter that this new place didn't seem real. It didn't freak me out that the grass and the sky—the fucking sun—looked more like a kid's finger painting than something of this world. I didn't even give a shit that there was a guy on the other side of a tree that seemed like it came out of an animated Halloween special staring right at me with eyes that looked like black holes. I just figured it was part of the crazy-assed hallucinations I was having.

Fuck it—I'm free!

No blood—maybe it was all a dream. The thought made me laugh. It couldn't be true; I remembered how warm and slick her blood felt on my hands before waking up in this weird place too well for it to be my imagination, but go with it for a second. Maybe Felicia wasn't dead. Maybe I didn't even attack her—who gives a damn? All I care about right now is that she's gone, which means the shit is over.

Amidst all the screaming and whining, I laughed like I had never laughed before.

# CHAPTER THREE

I KNEW that life the way I knew it had irreversibly changed the moment I saw a corpse driving a car. I also knew I was tripping but not so hard that I didn't know a dead man when I saw one. The man behind the wheel of a red Subaru that had seen better days was middle-aged, and his chin sported fresh stubble. His old-fashioned wire-rimmed glasses were perched on his nose. There wasn't anything discernibly wrong with him, not at first glance. He looked like a regular guy driving around town on a sunny day. Except this 'regular guy' couldn't be driving around today or ever again for that matter. I knew that because my mom went to his funeral just a couple of days ago.

*Get your shit together, Carrie.*

I sat up taller, took a deep breath, and put both hands on the wheel, trying to shake off what had to be the result of some bad Spice. I'll never buy shit from that asshole Tyler again.

Mr. Ridley nodded as I coasted next to him, coming dangerously close to hitting the Subaru and giving it (and him) the burial it deserved. Some of the lines that had etched themselves in his face when he was alive had smoothed out, and his hair, lackluster at best before he collapsed in front of the library clutching his chest, had regained some body and even some color. There wasn't any green decomposing skin, no withered lips and rotted gums, nothing like that. Is this what zombies really look like? Wait, are zombies real and this is what happens? I had convinced myself that I was hallucinating somewhere along the way and was settling into the fantasy… and it was freaking me out fast. Do we just reanimate after we die and go on about our merry way? Shouldn't you move to a new town if you're going to do that? I mean, what if you bump into someone that knew you when you were alive—?

It was the wave that did me in.

Just a gentle flick of the wrist: an open-handed salute. It was so jovial, so natural. His hand seemed to glow. The sky behind him was the brightest, darkest blue I'd ever seen. It was like the night sky was backlit by a spotlight or something. It made the sky weird. Too blue. It was kind of like the color of the water you see when you're out in the middle of the ocean. That's how it looked on that cruise Mom and Dad took me on before I started high school. The water was so deep out there—it seemed like you would never find the bottom if you dropped anchor. I remember staring at it every day, getting more and more spooked. How could anyone survive out there? Who knows what lurks beneath the surface?

Blue, teal, turquoise, and midnight all rolled into one— that's what the color of the sky looked like. It was as wrong as Mr. Ridley was. His hand looked obscenely bright against it, but he didn't seem to notice. He just went on waving at me under the weirdest-looking sky I'd ever seen.

*Please don't smile.*

I don't think I can handle it if he smiles.

I didn't feel my car careen off the road and hit the turn-buckle because I was too busy staring at Mr. Ridley and the sky. The sky and Mr. Ridley. I passed out before the impact praying that Mr. Ridley didn't smile and show me his pointy teeth.

# CHAPTER FOUR

I DIDN'T KNOW I was looking for something new, but damn, he is gorgeous. Dirty blond, blue eyes, with abs that lead into the most perfect pelvic muscle I've ever seen up close. Australian accent on a velvety voice, barely legal, and eager. He's the polar opposite of any other man I've ever been with, but I'm not complaining. He takes his time and savors me like fine wine. I could listen to him moan all day long, and sometimes I do just that. He leaves me satisfied and crazy for more.

I'm so preoccupied with Dustin that I rarely even think of Jared anymore.

Dustin adores me. He says as much, but that's not how I know. It's when I catch him looking at me out of the corner of my eye that speaks volumes. His face goes through so many emotions at once, it's almost painful to watch. Love, admiration, obsession, lust. Fear. He wants this to last forever and doesn't know if it can.

He's beautiful and smart.

He loves the sun and lets it kiss his skin with zeal; watching him take off his shirt in its yellow glow is an exercise in restraint. He wants to marry me, but that will never be. Regardless of what happens between Jared and I, I would never go on record as being 21 years my husband's senior. Dustin just laughs when I say that. He says he'll push my wheelchair out to see the surf every day if that's what I want. Ah, my pretty. I think he really believes he would.

He met me on the beach today. Just ran by me with his board under his arm; I sensed him more than saw him until he had run several paces away. He threw a kiss over his shoulder and dove into the tumultuous sea, ready to enjoy the waves for as long as the sunlight held. I was content to watch him move in the water, read my book, and feel the breeze.

This had become my typical day, and I loved every minute of it.

Sometimes I wondered what was going on between us. Is this just a fling? How did this happen? There are so many things that I don't remember. I feel like I'm drunk on whatever this is—passion, lust, love? I don't remember when I decided I was going to cheat on Jared. We weren't having any problems. Life was the comfortable normal that marriages slip into over time. I know Jared as well as I know myself—does he know what I've been up to?

As I watched Dustin come out of the surf I can understand what caught my eye. Any woman would be hard pressed to not do a double take. But I never thought I'd cheat.

As Dustin came closer those thoughts were invaded by others, ones that make me shift in my seat. It made the worries seem unimportant. For now.

I felt my cheeks get hot as he stood over me. His lopsided smile was my undoing. I felt flutters deep in my belly and had to look away. This is one hell of a forty-something-woman-going-through-a-midlife-crisis checklist item, that's for sure.

Dustin laid me down on the sand. He kissed my eyelids, my cheekbones, my nose, my mouth. His touch, made rough by the white sand, still managed to raise goose bumps on my skin. He stretched my arms overhead, clasped one hand in his, palm to palm, fingers interlaced like first loves often do, and traced a line from my elbow to waist with the other, watching his fingers as they moved. I could see the desire in his eyes as he looked at my body, could sense the control he struggled to keep over himself. He bit his lip to keep it at bay, his desire threatening to quicken his pace. He wanted to go slowly because he knew I liked it when he did, even though he felt like he couldn't wait any longer. He wanted to savor me, though his mouth watered. That realization affected me in a way I didn't expect. The tears that stung the corners of my eyes were real. Exhilaratingly real, and so very scary.

He guided himself inside me without ever letting go of my hand.

The sky looked incredible. Such a brilliant blue. I was trying to come up with the name for it; the name was just on the tip of my tongue when Dustin sent me over the edge. Then I started thinking about how I might never go home if this pretty young thing plans to fuck me like this every time.

And then I stopped thinking all together.

The last thing I saw before I woke up to the brilliant blue of that weird sky was the first thing I was looking for but couldn't find. Where is Dustin? I looked around taking in all the people scattered about in various stages of confusion but none of them kept my attention. But the sky did. It kept pulling my eyes away from task. Though the color was the same, it wasn't beautiful to me anymore. It was all encompassing and thick. Heavy. It seemed to bear down on me, as interested in crushing me as hovering above me. I felt its menace in every part of my body.

My clothes were the same, just a sundress and sandals,

still hiked up over my hips the way Dustin had left me. My skin looked the same, and I felt the same. But everything had changed.

"Dustin?"

I whispered his name at first, not wanting to draw the attention of the others, though that might have been impossible anyway.

I was lying in a tree that was close to the ground. It was very much like the Divi Divi trees that grow in Aruba with their affected lean and gnarled roots. My toes scraped the ground from my perch, but the rest of my body was enclosed in the tree as though I was sitting in its mouth. And the leaves were so green. Breathtakingly green. The most intensely bright green I had ever seen before. The tree, the whole place, was alive in a way that nature wasn't intended to be. I felt like a cricket veering too close to a Venus Flytrap.

I pried myself out of the tree's grip and stood on grass that crunched underfoot. "Dustin?" I said again, panic invading my voice. He shouldn't be here—I know that now. More than anything I hoped he wasn't here. That sweet man who loved me right when I needed it shouldn't have to endure this. I didn't want to know what his face looked like in the light of the harsh crayon sun that hung overhead like a weight.

It dawned on me that this is exactly where I belonged. It felt like some kind of reverse Rapture. All the good people stayed on Earth and the bad ones—the ones who cheated and didn't think twice about their husbands—were sent to hell. Because this is hell, right?

It certainly feels like it.

I saw him approaching in the distance and wondered about his size. Jared was a big man, sure, but something about him seemed disproportionate somehow. And his gait—it was too deliberate. Almost like he was trying too hard to put one foot in front of the other. I shook my head in resignation. This is what I deserve, isn't it? Not Dustin but Jared— new and improved… and sure to be mad as hell. I bought it and paid for it, indeed.

"Corinne, baby! Oh, thank God!"

The words were his, but the voice wasn't. But that's all right. As Jared's arms encircled me, pulling me into his soft, fleshy chest, the name of that color blue popped into my mind. Cerulean. That's what it was. The color of the Caribbean Sea transposed in the sky. My eyes fell onto the faces of people I don't know. Some of them were paralyzed with fear, and others in blissful ignorance of what lies ahead. I'm too sad to be scared even though Jared's embrace felt more like a vise.

# CHAPTER FIVE

HAZY.

That's what it seemed like but not what it was.

Maybe my vision was hazy—maybe my mind. I wanted to go back to sleep. But I hadn't been sleeping, had I?

Not really.

Wishing for it, maybe. Sleep was all I wanted to do these days. Being awake was a chore; the constant hemming and hawing about trivial things that most people my age engage in had started to grate on my nerves a long time ago. I wanted to shut all of that nonsense out. I did everything I could to make it go away, short of the final step.

Is that what this was? Had I finally gotten rid of that Catholic guilt and found the balls to do what needed to be done? Caroline would be disappointed to see me this way, if seeing the dead again is what really happens when all is said and done. She might say, in that exasperated tone she reserved just for me, 'Oh, Edward,' and give me a good smack to prove that point. But I would take it if it meant being with her again. I'd give anything to hear the sound of her voice again.

What took me so long to do it? When Caroline died all those years ago I thought I would go after her. I was sick. Hell, I had been sick first, so it made sense. But then my heart disease got under control (the doctors kept referring to my cluster of heart attacks as blips on my screen), and my health rebounded—not all the way, but enough to keep me kicking. The doctors patted each other on the back; the kids cheered and hugged, but I sulked. I pulled away, stayed home more because that's where it was quiet. I stopped seeing the doctor because I wanted whatever they did to be undone. I wanted to go with Caroline. Life without her wasn't much of a life at all.

But that was eight years ago. Eight years of living in the shadows, watching trash TV, crying over old pictures, only speaking to the kids when they pressed the issue: avoiding life. They knew what was going on—Robbie said he'd help me do it if I really wanted to. But I couldn't saddle him with that for the rest of his life. My good boy would suffer, too, and I didn't want that to happen.

I learned something over those eight years. You can't will death. It'll come when it's good and ready and not a moment before.

I remember going to bed with Caroline and the kids on my mind. I was thinking about an outing at the lake up in Greenbrier, Maryland, from 40 years ago. The sun was shining, and a cool breeze ruffled my hair. I could feel warmth on my cheeks even in the darkness of the one room I lived out of anymore. I couldn't make myself walk around the house much. Too many ghosts occupying the rooms.

I don't remember deciding to do it. I had contemplated the ways a million times—pills seemed the easiest. The thought of shooting myself and not dying made me sick to my stomach. I didn't think I could take a knife to myself, and I wasn't about to jump off anything. Pills I could do. I'd just take all the doses of Tambocor that I missed and let my heart literally skip a beat. It would be quick. Not painless, but that's not what I'm looking for.

But then this happened.

I looked around at the landscape I woke up to. It was beautiful, yet odd in a way that frightened me. My house was gone. In fact, I couldn't see any houses at all. There were too many people around, people who were paying attention to everyone else but trying to look like they weren't. And the sky. There was something wrong with the sky. It was like a kid's coloring page—the colors were too bright and unrealistic. And harsh.

Where the hell is Caroline?

If this is what I think it is, and I've checked out of life once and for all, why isn't she here to greet me? She can't still be mad that I put her in a home, not after all these years… could she?

Some people were crying quietly. Some cried out loud with such gut wrenching wails they made my hair stand on end. Some got angry, demanding an answer, a reason for being in this new place—they stood shouting into the open air. Others hugged themselves against the outside world. Me, I just sat and watched. I didn't think I had enough control over myself to do anything else.

# CHAPTER SIX

THE ROOM WAS alive for the first time since the beginning, buzzing and beeping accompanied by loud, fast-talking nurses and doctors. There was a lot of reaching, running, and commotion. And then nothing. No movement, no people, no noise.

Dr. Mitchell stood in the middle of the room, his vantage point allowing a view of all of them. Jennifer, 28. Brandon, 33. Carrie, 19. Corinne, 41. Edward, 77. All wheeled into the large room that would end up being their death chamber within minutes of each other. All gone at virtually the same time.

The hallucinogen had been injected into each patient's IV in tandem. Brain scans for each of them showed hyperactivity spikes and relaxed rhythm at the same pace. They seemed to enter the new sphere, a place designed to comfort them as they awaited their deaths, at the same time also. Cerulean Fields was his life's work: a utopia for the dying. It was supposed to give them peace at the end instead of pain, a loss of dignity, and fear.

But it didn't. It couldn't have. In the end they were all

writhing, fighting, clawing at the air. Something chased them to their death over there. Something unexpected.

He looked at the pictures of his patients that were posted on their bedside tables and felt a sadness well in him that he had dreaded from the beginning of the research. He had never met them; by the time they arrived at the facility their induced comas had already taken effect. He didn't want to know them, didn't want to see their eyes. That would have just complicated things.

The pictures showed each of his patients in the prime of their lives, their smiling faces a testament to their health in contrast to their present situation. Edward stood tall and confident, muscular in the way that men who enjoyed the outdoors were. His son Robert said that Edward had been an avid camper, taking the kids into the woods every summer. Robert couldn't bear to see his father like this, so frail and thin. It took everything he had to visit every week.

Jennifer's picture didn't look like her at all—the stroke paralyzed her entire left side and aged her overnight. Brandon's picture was of him out at a lake. You could only see his profile but that's the only image that his girlfriend would bring. She only came to visit once and didn't stay long. Carrie's picture was haunting. It showed a sweet little high school kid with her whole life ahead of her. It was Carrie before the drugs and the self-imposed isolation. It was Carrie before the accident.

Corinne was the true beauty in the bunch. Dr. Mitchell's affinity for her was evident from the start. He could see a beautiful woman beneath the graying skin. Looking at her grounded him, made him see the patients as people instead of research specimens. Every time he looked at the picture of her on the beach with her sarong flowing in the wind revealing slender, shapely legs, he grew more attached. Her caramel skin, sun-kissed in the picture, seemed to glow. She radiated confidence even before the vast sea in front of her.

He wished he knew her before the cancer ravaged her body, before chemotherapy stole her hair, before her eyes closed forever. If they had met in a coffee shop, would she have noticed him? Would she order a Chai tea latte and turn to see him staring at her? Would she smile the same way she did in the picture, joyful and provocative, and make his knees buckle? If they met on a crowded street would she be interested in him, or would his blue eyes not be her cup of tea? Sometimes he got angry because he would never have the chance to find out.

Sometimes he touched Corinne's hand when he thought of what could have been, wanting to feel her skin next to his own. He interlaced their fingers when the fantasy was particularly compelling, gingerly holding her paper-thin skin against his, gaining closer contact in the most appropriate way possible even though, in his mind, they moved from hugging to kissing to more. He imagined how he would caress her skin, run his hands through her hair, kiss her beautiful full lips—lips that had only been parted to brace a feeding tube since he had known her. Dr. Mitchell spoke to her about the places they would have gone if they had the chance, sharing a fantasy that could never come true with a woman he wasn't entirely sure could hear him. He felt like a kid talking about his hopes and dreams. Corinne made him giddy in a way that he hadn't been since he was 20 years old. He reveled in a past they never shared and mourned a future that would never be. Many times he wondered how life could be so cruel to show him true love in the touch of a dying woman.

Dr. Mitchell looked at Corrine, studied her. This would be the last time he saw her. Once he left the room she shared with the other patients their connection would be lost. He was not ready to say goodbye.

He puttered around the room a bit more, cleaning up, wasting time, trying to prepare himself for the inevitable. Soon the families would be notified, and the bodies would be claimed. They would be gone within hours. Corrine would be gone forever.

The thought was unbearable.

"Dr. Mitchell, we need your signature on the files."

The nurse's voice barely registered to him. The only sound he could hear was waves crashing on the shore.

"Dustin?"

The nurse had moved close enough to touch his arm. He had to restrain himself from shaking her hand off. She handed him the folders and left him alone. He saw the concern in her eyes as she did, but she was mercifully silent.

He touched Corinne's hand one last time. It was still warm. Perhaps that was the worst part.

# ANSWERING MACHINE

I GOT a call from a friend today. She wanted to go out for breakfast to that place she likes. Wanted to eat pancakes with blueberry syrup and scrambled eggs with cheese. And grits. She always wants grits. That's what she said on my answering machine, the hulking dinosaur that still sits on my hall table next to the phone. She calls me old school for keeping it. Says I'm dating myself by even having it around. Maybe she's right. But there's nothing wrong with a little old school every now and then.

She sounded so perky, so excited. Something must be going right in her life. That's good. Maybe she finished the project she's been agonizing over for months, trying to get the right angle, form the right words. She was pumped up. Proud. And good for her. I listened to her voice with a wistfulness I didn't expect to feel. I'm happy for her, but more than happiness, I feel content. Like hearing that she is doing well today means she will do well forever. That's silly, I know. Part of me knows that, at least. But maybe forever is today. And that's not so silly after all.

My friend stopped talking before I stopped listening so I

heard everything that came after: the wet sliding sound, the mucous-laden snorts that got louder and louder. I heard the wheezing—that was the worst for me, that sick, terrible sound emanating from the depths of the thing's lungs—the labored breathing. I thought I might be able to get away, thought I could borrow some of that "I am so awesome" vibe my friend just left on my answering machine, but I couldn't. Not now, when my leg, mangled to the bone, sits tied to the hall table leg. The table, God love it, is on its back now after my fruitless kicking, pulling, wrenching episode. Any energy I had was used up in trying to get away the first time.

Or was that the second?

I lost track.

The smell of pancakes with blueberry syrup was a figment of my imagination, I knew. Just a jab, a "you wish you could" zinger pushed up by my mind's evil eye. Or was it? Couldn't it be that the smell from my memory was given to me as a gift? One to occupy me while the thing slurping, shuffling, and, dear God, wheezing had its way? Maybe so. I don't know. In a different world I would think so. But as the wheezing thing stepped on the answering machine and played my friend's cheerful chirping again, I had my doubts.

# OBSERVATIONS AT THE SUPERMARKET

Cheddar cheese.

Swiss cheese.

Jack cheese.

Block.

Shredded.

She's standing next to me, staring at the cheese like she doesn't know which one to get.

Finely shredded.

Shredded—as in plain old.

The corner of her eye twitches—actually shudders, like wind causing the surface of standing water to ripple... like a shiver from a cold breeze.

Made with 2% or whole milk—come on, I urge silently from my perch next to her, in front of the canned pastry tubes, the ones you need only bang on the side of your counter to make the dough explode inside them... the ones that could put your eye out if you weren't careful... come on, I press with my eyes if not my voice, live a little.

Her eyes cascade down the packages of processed gunk—

that weird canned stuff, those perfect American cheese squares wrapped in plastic. She tripped over the bleu cheese, the goat cheese, the queso fresco, seeing but not seeing, knowing but not caring. Oh yes, she knows I'm watching her. She sees me from the corner of her eye even as it twitch-twitch-twitches.

She licks her lips when I shift from the balls of my feet to the heel. Balls to heels. Back and forth. Back...

Cottage cheese.

Cream cheese.

How about goat cheese, hmm? Creamy and white. Soft like a cotton ball against a splintering table. Soft, unlike its overripe sister, brie. Soft like waiting skin in the warmth of the noonday sun.

Soft.

Supple.

Pliant.

Ricotta cheese.

Her lips part to reveal the bottoms of blackened teeth; ridged, the mamelons unsmoothed, unnaturally prominent.

Jagged enough to cut her skin.

In fact, I was sure she had cut her tongue, her finger, and anything else that had had come into contact with those teeth many a time. And just as I knew that, I knew she liked it too.

Colby cheese.

Monterey Jack.

Muenster.

She snickered.

She bit her bottom lip.

A trickle of blood blossomed against her flesh, rising like a fount, spreading, bubbling over.

Red.

Bright.

Dark.

Dead.

I knew it.

I need cheese.

Suddenly I need cheese more than I've ever needed anything before.

What do I want today? What's my fancy? Maybe a mix like Jalapeño Jack for my spicy burger or the gimmicky Mexican blend, which is just a mix of some regular old cheese bagged together with the illusory "quesadilla cheese" (yeah, I see you). Or maybe I need some old-fashioned mold in the form of Neufchâtel or maybe the saucy not cheese Velveeta for the nachos I didn't know I wanted.

My mouth is open and I don't know why.

She can hear me breathing.

A smile plays at the corner of her lips as she looks at me—looks right at me—without ever turning her head.

Just one beady little eye.

Parmesan.

Asiago.

I reach out to grab something, anything.

I beat her to it, her taloned hand jutting out a fraction of a second after mine to land on the thin skin that covered the bones on the back of my hand... metacarpal bones, fragile bones like those of a baby's, every detail exposed under the skin, protruding like a skeleton's—brittle, flimsy: weak.

A fraction of a second.

Long enough for me to wonder if I would ever get to taste the fresh mozzarella my hand had landed on, little balls of the stuff wet in the package, moving around like eyeballs in a sensory bowl—long enough for me to wish I hadn't—

Eggs.

Eyeballs in a sensory bowl are usually made of boiled eggs.

Eggs.

Brown.

Farm raised.

Quail-

# UPPERVILLE

UPPERVILLE. The town where all the inhabitants are family. The town where nobody leaves because the world doesn't exist past the city limits. The town I'm from.

Getting out was always a priority for me. The streams that border the town, the well that stood in our backyard, all smelled stagnant to me. Like rot. Like death. I didn't want to be consumed, to be sucked into the very ground like it was quicksand or the hungry mouth of a Venus Flytrap. I didn't want to live and die only knowing Upperville's monotony, with its white picket fences and its picturesque winding roads. "Upperville, the sleepy hollow less than an hour from the city," it had been called in some magazine years ago. To me it was more like "Upperville, town of the damned." So I left. I jumped on 66 and made for the city. Washington, DC.

I even wrote an article about it, one of my first features at the paper before I got moved up. "The Decline of Rural America," I called it, proudly typing Susan McCoy in the byline. I had to rewrite it so it didn't smack of Upperville bashing, not because I cared what the people back home thought—I didn't think they would get the paper anyway,

55

and if they did, they wouldn't read it—but because I wanted to make a good impression at my new job. When the paper came out there were grumblings, Mother said in her usual, I-just-happened-to-hear-it way. But there were always grumblings, at least, as far as I was concerned. People never seemed to like me or the things I did. Mother said it had more to do with her than it did with me, but she would never explain it. And she would never leave, no matter how much I begged. She said she was bound to the land just like my soul was bound to be free. I never listened when she started talking that way. Instead it strengthened my determination to get out. If that's what Upperville did to you, I didn't want any part of it. Sometimes Mother acted as kooky as the rest of them did. I wasn't going to let that happen to me.

I hate Upperville with a passion.

And now I'm going back.

Even my mother's death hadn't brought me back to Suckerville. I had her body shipped to DC and forced anyone who wanted to pay their respects to leave their comfort zones and come to me. No one did. I found out later they held an informal service over my mother's body at the morgue. The coroner had lived in Upperville all his life, so even though it was against the rules, he lit a candle in front of mother's body on the slab along with the rest of them.

But now Bobby Zucker was dead. I had to go back.

The drive was over before I knew it. Memories of Bobby and me stealing kisses behind the school and copping feels in the cab of his father's pickup flooded my mind, wiping away the road and replacing it with his face. He was my first kiss, my first lover, my first love. I lived and breathed him until I left for college. He stayed behind to work at his father's hardware store. I begged him to come with me, to leave Upperville and start a life with me in the city. But he didn't. As the years passed and Mother told me about Bobby's life—

sending me the invitation Bobby gave her for his wedding to Mary Lou Kramer (a cowgirl if there ever was one), giving me baby pictures when his children were born—I couldn't believe I had been so wrong about him. He wasn't the person I thought he was, wasn't the free spirit who thought for himself and did what he wanted to do in life. He was just like the rest of them in Upperville: a drone.

But I never forgot about him.

Even with all the dating I did, all the near misses, I never forgot about Bobby. I always wondered what it would have been like had he left Upperville and come with me. He might have been a lawyer, like he wanted to be. He might have had a successful practice in Northwest DC, might have been a real player. We might have been happy.

But now he's dead.

Carlene, my mother's best friend and the only other person in Upperville who knew how to reach me, said that he fell from a ladder and hit his head. She said he never regained consciousness, using a sympathetic tone that made it seem like that was for the best. But it wasn't. The Bobby I knew would have wanted to wake up and say goodbye to his family and friends, would have wanted one last moment to see the sun from his window. But I kept that to myself. There was no sense in upsetting Carlene's "Uppervillian" logic, her untested, all-knowing sensibility.

Damn him for making me come back.

Damn him for not coming with me.

The main road—aptly named Main Street—looked the same as it had when I took it out of town twenty-one years ago. Same old stores, looking the worse for wear in the diminishing light, the same old church at the end of the badly pocked street. People went about their normal routine as I drove by, talking with each other in the entrance to the post office while scratching at their oversized, dirty overalls and plaid shirts, tipping their hat to the old woman who strolled past. Doing nothing. I've seen it all before. It hurt to think that Bobby had become one of them.

The funeral home was off a side street with even more cars lined up than on Main. People had come to pay their respects. Bobby must have been well-liked, and why wouldn't he be? He was one of the most handsome kids in school, one of the most grounded people I had ever met. I bet he was a magnet, someone who the cowpokes wanted to be around. It made them feel better about themselves. And now that beacon was gone.

That's what he was, wasn't he? A beacon that had called me back to a place I swore I'd never step foot in again.

With a deep breath, I walked into the funeral home. It was suitably muted, as were most places like that—no sense in turning up the lights so you can see the death mask in plain view.

I didn't recognize Carlene when she approached me. "Susan? Is that you? My God, you look so different!" she cackled louder than she should have in a funeral home.

"Carlene. It's great to see you!" I lied. I didn't care if I ever saw her again. Bobby was the only person I cared about in that godforsaken town. And now he was gone.

Two other people milled behind her, openly listening to our exchange. "Well, you remember Karen Whitetower and Vern Glover, don't you?"

I nodded my greeting, desperately wanting to get away from them.

"I bet you're anxious to see Bobby, then," she said, her face twisting in a sly smile. "I know how close you two were."

Something about her troubled me.

"He's right in there," she said, turning my shoulders and nudging me toward the room where Bobby's body lay. "Go on," she urged, flashing her too-sweet smile.

The whole drive there all I wanted to do was see him, see that Bobby was dead with my own eyes, but now that I was there, in the place where he was laid out, I was afraid. Seeing him would mean that it was really over. Everything we had ever shared was done, gone, finished. Even when he got married, I thought there might be a little something left, something we might grab onto later in life. But now that he was dead, there would be no chance of that. I was terrified.

"Go on, Susan," Carlene said, her voice more urgent this time. "Go in and see Bobby."

I started walking before I allowed my thoughts to register. Carlene's behavior, her expressions, everything about her bothered me. Why did she care if I went in to see Bobby? Why did it have to be so rushed? I brushed the concern away, chalking it up to my nervousness. I was, after all, at my first love's funeral. Maybe I was a little sensitive.

I heard the whispering among the people who ringed the corridor—

"That's Lizzie's girl, isn't it?"

"She ain't been back here for twenty years!"

"Not even for her mother's funeral."

I turned to see who made that comment, but no one met me eye to eye. Funeral? I had mother's funeral in DC. If they were talking about their cultish sendoff in the morgue, fine. But they said funeral. Had they held a service that I missed? Anger welled within me, swirling inside my stomach. How dare they not let me know about something like that? *I'll have to ask Carlene about that before I leave*, I thought as I turned their whispers around in my head. I approached Bobby's casket at a snail's pace.

It was open, with a yellowish light shining on the place where Bobby's head should have rested. But he wasn't there. I didn't see what I expected to see, Bobby with his eyes closed and the lids pulled a little too tightly over the eyes to look natural, Bobby with makeup dusting his temples to cover the greenish gray tint his flesh had taken in death, Bobby whose glued lips looked nothing like the soft ones I had kissed so long ago. I picked up my pace, ignoring the voice in my mind that insisted that Bob's body laid lower than usual, that his wife must have sprung for the deluxe model casket, high walls, plush satin and all.

*No casket is that deep*, a stronger, more resilient version of my own voice admonished.

He wasn't there.

The casket was empty, its silk bedding untouched. As I turned to ask the nearest Upperville moron what was going on, I caught sight of a stocky man, about six feet tall with dusty brown hair and twinkling brown eyes. Bobby. He was older, but I'd know his face anywhere.

"Bobby, what—?" I started to ask him. His smile spread into a wild grin as I shrank against the casket. I never saw who hit me in the back of the head, never even felt the blow. The blood running down my neck felt warm, calming as I rested my head on the pillow and looked at Bobby. I didn't feel them hoist my legs over the side of the casket, didn't hear them laugh and jeer, condemning me for leaving as I bled out. Only the touch of Bobby's lips on mine registered. When he parted my lips and put his tongue in my mouth I closed my eyes like I did when we were kids.

# GOLDENROD SUN

So BEAUTIFUL, that time just before twilight, when the sun sits low in the sky. Its rays cascade a brilliant hue for a time; like looking through yellow lenses. Her eyes absorbed the light illuminating everything around her, sucking it into the blackness that was creeping in, suffocating it as a drowning swimmer overtakes his rescuer. But beautiful was she in that goldenrod sun, if only for a time.

# CHURCH

The windows are blacked out, but there is still the faintest glimmer of light coming from inside.

I'm waiting on the steps, unsure if something has changed and the meeting is off. Yvette told me to come on time, so I did. Going to church after hours (or at all, if I'm being honest) had never been my thing, but I did it for her. I love her. I want her to be my wife, and if coming to church to meet her Bible study group was what she wanted, I would do it. What could it hurt? Lord knows I have enough to make up for, so maybe this is a start.

If I can ever get inside.

There's no wind out here. Nothing at all—not even the little something that barely flips your hair. It's still and quiet. And I am standing here alone.

My watch says it's already 10 minutes after. People should be parked here and ready to receive the Word—that's what Yvette would call it. I say they're ready to get their daily fix. Maybe that's the wrong way to think about it. Maybe that's why I haven't had the guts to stay away from Nicole yet, or to ask Yvette for that matter. Maybe I am thinking about this thing all wrong. Maybe when I get inside I can—

The glimmer in the window, the one that was way back in the recesses of the room a second ago, is now right in the front window, hovering next to the chipped white paint frame. I can't tell if it's inside or outside, but it doesn't matter. Not really. There are more of them now, more than just the one hovering in the corner. There are so many I can almost see...

# DESTINY

---

"IF WE WERE MEANT to be together, you'll find me."

That's what she said, though she never thought it would be *this* way... or did she? Maybe she did, and this was the culmination of her plan laid carefully down throughout the years, hidden in the shadows of truth or some such bullshit. Maybe she had wanted me to come here like this, stumbling and thirsty, wanting. She always liked to keep me wanting, didn't she? Hoping she would see me, desire me, crave me the way I craved her. As I sit her, dying to look upon her face once more, it is more of the same. Me wanting. Her laughing. The story of my life.

It had always been her and me, even when there were others around, others involved, others between us. To say that wasn't true would be to lie, and she knew that as much as I did. She cut herself, and I bled, it was as simple as that, except now... most markedly now, hmm? Her grand plans come to bear in the most amazing of ways.

"If we were meant to be together, you'll find me," she said as she backed out of the door, walking away with just the clothes on her back, saying goodbye to me forever. After I loved her, after I cherished her, after I drove myself mad trying to please her. Still she left without so much as a back-ward glance once the words had come out of her mouth, leaving me to stare at the open door as if waiting for her to return.

That was ten years ago.

Ten years ago to the day.

Could I have lasted longer? Maybe. Should I have? No. There is no should, would, could when it comes to her, at least not for me... except this—that I *should* do what I desire when it comes to her because she *would* have no other way.

Will she watch me come to her? Wait for me to shut my eyes in bliss before she graces my mouth with a kiss, her hot breath tantalizing me to slip deeper and deeper into her? I wonder as my call swirls bitterly on my tongue. I close my eyes, giving in to the very thing my body wants least to do but is compelled to because we are so very tired. But in that acquiescence comes familiarity, the sweet sound of laughter given to raspy ruin.

It rubs.

It burns.

"My darling," I whisper, the shuddering breath pulled from me relentlessly, lovingly: definitively. "I found you."

# ONCE A MONTH

Gasping awake… it's a thing.

Damien found himself sitting bolt upright with the remnants of said gasp in his ears, chest heaving, a thin sheen of sweat coating his brow. It was still dark, and the house was relatively quiet. He could make out the muffled sound of music from his older brother's room—even through the closed door, he was still able to hear the hook of Lil Watts' latest track, the one that bit off Juice WRLD's last album so much Damien couldn't stand to listen to it. It was loud—too loud—and if their mother woke up, Jared would have a problem, but Damien was thankful for it. It was normal. It was expected. It was the only thing that let Damien know he was really real.

*Come on, man.*

*Chill.*

Damien focused on controlling his breath. He picked up his phone.

3:38 a.m.

He sucked his teeth.

When was the last time he had been up at that time? Why

was he even up now? Damien wracked his brain, trying to remember the dream he was having before he woke up, trying to figure out what had bothered him so much that he found himself looking around his room in search of some-thing familiar just to be sure he had resurfaced in the right place. Had he been running? He was sweaty, so maybe. Had he been afraid? It seemed like he might have been. But of what?

Vampires and werewolves and voodoo priestesses making zombies. It had been Chris's turn to pick the movie for their Netflix Party that night, and he always chose horror. Even with *Hobbs & Shaw* or restarting the Marvel Universe—who doesn't like a little *Iron Man?*—on the table, he still went with some creepy foreign flick with demons that none of them could pronounce. Damien had watched. He wasn't going to wuss out, not with 10 of his friends active in the chat. He watched without interruption, even as it got later and later because his parents had become a little more lenient during the pandemic and staying up longer wasn't an issue. Normally he would have had to go to bed right about when the ghost in the movie showed its face the first time. Damien would have had to get off the laptop long before that, the 'no technology after 9:30 p.m.' rule he had been so irritated about alive and well before the days of social distancing and wearing masks everywhere you went had become the norm. Now his mom didn't freak out if he was online late with his friends. Now his dad didn't make a big deal about him posting videos all the time, even if the rest of them were in the background. Because now everything was different. Now online life was real life.

So, Damien watched the movie, and now the images were burned in his head. Creepy ones filled with darkness and strange sounds coming from deep inside someone's throat. He had been thinking about how the sound that the pantry door made was just like that if it was opened really slow when he fell asleep... and then he found himself sitting straight up in bed with a scream threatening to spill from his lips to chase the gasp.

He listened.

Had anyone heard him?

Was his mother rolling over, swinging her feet to the floor to pad into his room and check on him? It had been a long time since that had happened, and if he had anything to do with it, it would never happen again. He was 13 now; they had celebrated his birthday crowded in front of the laptop for half the day, a virtual party with friends and family keeping him rooted in place at the kitchen table so his parents and brother could drop by and say hi to whoever was on screen. It was cool and really weird, and he hoped he didn't have to celebrate another birthday like that ever again. But still and all, he was 13, and he didn't need his mother coming to check on him to see if he had a nightmare like the one when he couldn't find his way out of his closet or the one where the ice cream truck driver had no face. Those dreams might have seemed silly to his teenaged self but they were legitimate nightmares, ones that had wrenched him from his sleep, ones that had caused him to scream his mother's name. Terribly dark nightmares. And that was what he'd had just then... wasn't it?

He listened closer. Holding his breath.

Nothing but Lil Watt's voice, muffled and low.

Good.

He ran a hand over his face and sighed. It was too early to just stay up and wait until morning like his irrational mind wanted to—it would just as soon not meet the thing that had woken him up again. Besides, schoolwork still had to be done—virtual school or not. It was the one thing his mom made a stink about, but if he got it done early in the day, she let him do what he wanted afterward. He didn't want to give her a reason to change that.

Damien sighed and laid back down, the covers sticking to him more now than before. He wriggled into his go-to sleep position and, taking a deep breath, slammed his eyes shut. He was going back to sleep. He was. It was going to happen.

...

His eyes opened without him wanting them to, moving on their own, his vision changing from the nothingness of the back of his eyelids to his bedroom even as he tried keep them closed.

Damien sighed, said something he would never admit to, and tried again, but he couldn't keep his eyes closed for longer than a few seconds. He looked at the clock, but what he saw didn't make much sense.

3:62 a.m.

Yeah, ok.

He rubbed his eyes, trying to clear them, was about to look at the clock again, when he heard laughter coming from his brother's room. Laughter over a beat. Loud laughter over a loud beat.

He sucked his teeth. It was too loud. His mom would definitely hear it if he kept it up, and she would crack down on music overnight, using earbuds, whatever she was in the mood for at the moment. That would trickle down to him too—he had suffered enough restrictions that his brother had earned to know it would, it definitely, absolutely would —and Damien didn't want that. He liked his life right now. Sure, not being able to go out and do the stuff he liked to do stank, and the Xbox was getting old, but for the most part, his parents were being cool about a lot more than they would have been pre-crazy world. But Jared might mess that up. Damien couldn't have that.

Damien got up from bed and raced to Jared's room

almost as if floating on air. He was trying to be quiet, stealthy, and quick. He was all of those things and more, he noticed, as he opened the door and found himself standing somewhere entirely different than expected instead of his brother's messy room. Instead of clothes strewn all over the floor, Damien saw a game cabinet, one of those old-time stand-up machines from the 80s where you shot a centipede and dodged spiders and hid under mushrooms while wasps dive-bombed you. Instead of colored LED lights rimming the ceiling—Jared's pandemic project—he saw a black-lit miniature golf course with colorful neon paintings on the walls.

"Wha-?" Damien started, speaking out loud in wonder as he took it all in. The arcade was busy; clumps of kids stood in the simulator line, others waited for the indoor bumper cars. His brother was standing with his friends laughing at something, and Damien was suddenly sure it was him. He looked down at himself, confident that he was standing in the arcade with his pajamas on or worse, naked, some sleep-walking gene awakening in him at the worst possible time. But no. He had on one of his favorite outfits, too, so that wasn't it. He touched his hair, remembering the COVID-cut his mother had tried to give him before just letting it grow, but no, his fade felt tight under his hand. It wasn't him. He couldn't stop himself from sighing in relief.

Damien turned his head to see who the poor, unfortunate soul was and saw the back of a girl with a huge mallet in her hand. She was standing in front of a tall pillar that had lights on both sides of it and a digital gauge in the center. It reminded Damien of the high striker that he saw at the trav-elling carnivals that used to set up camp in the far corner of the old mall's parking lot, only that one wasn't digital. It had a little piece of metal that, once you hit the pad with the mallet, would shoot up through the channel toward the bell waiting at the top. He used to beg his dad to hit it, to show everyone how strong he was, and once he even made the bell ring. He walked around the rest of the day with a smile on his face. He could feel a similar smile breaking out there now.

Because this girl... she was... wow.

She was dressed like everyone else was—jeans, a hoodie, Vans, but the jeans had lace patches on them and the hoodie was some kind tie-dye pattern in orange and yellow and red... maybe a sunburst or something... and the Vans were orange-on-orange checkerboard. Her hair was braided or twisted or whatever, cascading down her back before a hair tie caught it. She wasn't wearing anything that made her stand out, and he couldn't even see her face, but Damien knew somehow that she was amazing. She was fantastic. She was important.

"Hey," Damien heard from somewhere behind him, next to him, all around him, but he knew it wasn't directed at him. He knew that he wasn't supposed to answer; he wondered if he had said it himself, even. He looked at the girl and knew he wasn't supposed to look away—that if he did it would be the worst mistake of his life.

Time slowed down as she turned, the way the shopping carts in the supermarket slowed and sometimes stuck when they encountered a rock in their path. It took forever, this turning around, and he thought he might scream if she didn't get it over with already, if she didn't turn around all the way so he could see her face.

Then he realized he was still looking... still looking at a girl he didn't know—who didn't even know he was standing there. And he wanted to avert his eyes, he wanted to look somewhere else... anywhere else. Because if she turned around and caught him staring at her she might... she might...what *would* she do?

She turned…

Her eyes were oval-shaped and chocolate brown with long eyelashes that curled at the ends and looked like she was wearing makeup on them but she wasn't, and he didn't understand because he had never noticed anything like that about anyone before, and he wondered if she noticed that he was still staring because he was and –

"…and?" Chris said, cramming chips into his mouth, one hand on the Xbox controller, Damien's voice a little louder in his ear than he wanted it to be but, his headset was spotty to begin with, so whatever. The tournament was coming up, and Damien had just started talking about real stuff in the practice room. Chris hoped they didn't have to postpone.

"That's it, man. Then I woke up." Damien still sounded tired but at 1:00 p.m., he had been up for an hour already.

"You only saw her eyes, though? How could you only see one part of her face?" Chris asked incredulously. The way Damien was describing it, it was if her face had scrolled down like an unravelling roll of paper and then gotten stuck right under the eyes.

"It was like her nose and mouth were like, fuzzed out? I don't know how else to explain it. It was like they weren't there."

"That's creepy."

Damien's response was noncommittal, nothing more than a grunt, really. Because while he understood why Chris might think it sounded creepy, he remembered how he felt when he saw her, how he knew he was supposed to be standing there right there, right then. Nothing about it had been creepy at all.

"… right? Like that lucid dream thing we learned about in class. But you went to the *arcade*? I mean, if I could pick where I went in my dreams I'd go to a Ferrari dealership and test drive one," Chris said and Damien could see him

72

weaving the Ferrari he was going to use in the tournament onscreen as he spoke. "Or maybe Wakanda."

"Please tell me you're joking," Damien groaned, wondering how much of what his best friend had been saying he'd missed as memories of some dude who had tattooed the word 'Wakanda' in glowing ink on the inside of his lip flooded his head.

"What?" Chris asked, his car zigzagging on the track, virtually warming up the tires for the race.

"It's not real, my guy."

"Yeah, but none of it is. It's a dream. So, why not do something you can't do in real life?"

Chris snickered under his breath, but it was still loud and clear in Damien's headset.

"This dude went to the *arcade*."

"Whatever, man," he said, ready to stop talking about last night's dream or the girl or the weirdness that surrounded her. But he didn't forget. Even as they entered the tournament and summarily whipped two teams back to back, he didn't forget.

An article out of some online magazine out of the UK said he should go to sleep on a schedule, so he did. A medical reference said he could tell himself he was going to have a lucid dream and that suggestion might work after a while. A guy he met in an online gaming meet-up asked him how he didn't know *this* wasn't the actual dream and while that was weird, continued conversation revealed some ways to check, and that constantly practicing those would help him if he was ever able to get back into that state. This garnered a fair amount of laughter from Jared, though, so Damien kept his practicing down to a minimum. He even gave up electronics right before bed because a doctor in Australia said it could help induce lucid dreams.

He tried.

And tried.

And tried.

Almost gave up.

But then he remembered her eyes.

And tried again.

\* \* \*

"No, that's water. You can live like 11 days without sleep."

"But what actually kills you? How do you die from not sleeping? I don't understand."

Damien was raising his voice but he didn't mean to. It was just that everything was so quiet in the house. His mother and father were in bed, and Jared had actually come to his room to talk. Even in his fatigue-induced haze, or perhaps because of it, he realized that it had been a long time since he and his brother had just talked without it being orchestrated by their parents.

Jared didn't pull any punches. He told Damien he looked like he hadn't slept in days, told him that he knew he had taken some of his Red Bull stash, and could smell the coffee on his breath. Damien didn't have the energy to argue.

"I don't know, man," Jared answered, rubbing the back of his neck. *He* was tired, so he knew his brother was... in fact, he felt like if they were quiet for a few minutes he would fall asleep right there. Why wouldn't Damien? He could see that he wanted to—he was almost asleep on his feet. What was stopping him?

"There's a word for it," Jared continued, looking at Damien through red, scratchy eyes. "Something that means you stop being able to figure out what is real and what isn't."

"Yeah, derealization, I know," Damien said irritably. He pressed his finger into his opposite palm, driving his nail into the skin, watching what happened intently. If his finger stayed on the outside it was ok, everything was ok because he knew that world, knew what should happen in it. If his finger went through...

That guy in the meet-up told him this would help... said it was a surefire way to know...

A crescent moon-shaped indent formed on the inside of his hand.

He sighed.

"Still awake... I hope."

Jared stared at his little brother, unable to find words to help, unable to ask anything except why.

"I-I can't go back," Damien said, asking the unanswered question in Jared's eyes. "I can't see her again because... because she might..."

Damien's shoulders slumped, and he covered his eyes with his hand. Jared sat up in his chair, leaning toward his brother who had never acted like this before, had never frightened him so badly before.

He was quiet.

Jared waited until he could wait no longer.

"She..? She who? She might what? Come on, D. Tell me."

"I saw her again, a couple times after that day," Damien started. "At first we just played games. We would go away from the others—you were there—and we would play the old games, you know the ones Mom and Dad like. She was good at Frogger. Really good. She could get on those logs faster than I could. Then we would shoot hoops, and I would beat her, but not all the time. She was good at that too. In the beginning it was just like that. We would play games and laugh and then I would wake up and try to get back in but I couldn't. But then I *could* get in, and it was all good. She was always right there waiting for me to come back in. But then she wasn't her anymore."

"What do you mean?" Jared wasn't tired anymore. He was somewhere between confused and scared to death.

"She was different. Older. But she still smiled at me. And once I could see her whole face I realized she was the most beautiful woman I had ever seen. And she would take my hand and run with me and look up to me because I wasn't really me anymore either, and then we were watching a sunset and then we were holding hands on the beach. Then she was smiling with a baby in her arms and then she was crying in some kind of auditorium. And she was older every time and still beautiful to me. I could feel myself smiling back at her and laughing with her and crying too. I tried to go in all the time but could only get in every once in a while. I guess that article was true—they said once a month if you're lucky. But I don't know if this is luck or what because she…"

Damien took a deep breath and shook his head, unable to meet his brother's eyes.

"She… the last time I saw her she was old. Really old. And she was looking at me differently. She was looking *down* at me, man…"

Damien didn't say anything else because from somewhere behind him, next to him, all around him, he heard someone speaking… just one word… but as clear as a bell.

"Hey."

The girl in front of him, dressed in a bright colored hoodie sporting bantu knots was standing in front of Space Invaders Frenzy. He could hear the rapid-fire shooting coming from The Walking Dead arcade game next to them, could hear people laughing and talking all over the place, and it all felt so normal. People were getting back to normal and that was good. It had been a long time since people had been able to go out and do something as simple as playing games in an arcade. Damien was suddenly happy to be there, happier than he had ever been to be anywhere in his whole life.

Except for the ringing in his ears, everything was fine.

The girl turned around, head haloed by flashing game lights. Her face mask, a homemade tie-dye job in yellow and orange and red, had one word written in the center in fancy script:

*Forever*

# MINE

----

FIVE-TEN, golden skin, longish black hair, brown eyes, thin nose, high cheekbones, plump lips, medium build, rounded shoulders, hairless chest, tan nipples. Inny. Above average-sized member. Muscular thighs. Muscular calves. Average-sized feet.

Pretty.

She took a deep breath; this had to be done right the first time.

She opened his sleeve, watched as his hair fell out of place to cover one eye.

Very pretty.

"You don't want to look some more? You've only seen the one," he said from the back of the store, but she ignored him. She didn't need to see any others. This was the one.

"What kind of voice box does this one have?" Her voice sounded breathy, even to herself.

"Whatever you want," he said, still calling to her from somewhere else, some unseen perch she imagined was littered with food wrappers and smeared with lithium grease. "Tenor, bass, high-pitched, squeaky—whatever you like."

He sounded like he was chewing a particularly tough piece of meat; she could hear the saliva sloshing around in his mouth.

"What's there now?"

Impatient.

"A74?"

Keys clicking.

Spit sloshing.

She ran a hand along his thigh, just at the knee, where the muscle was taut. Good to touch.

"That one's a baritone."

Smooth, silky, warm.

Yes.

"I'll take it."

She looked up at him, his lips slightly pouty, straight face slightly stern. Resting bitch face.

Perfect.

Paid.

Prepped.

Alone in the back room. The staging room. Could try him out here if she wanted, he said. Private, private except for the peep holes he had likely drilled in every wall.

She looked at her phone one more time to make sure she knew what to say. The rules said she couldn't read it from the screen: it had to be recited from memory. The rules said she could only say it once and that if she made any mistakes, it wouldn't work, not on this one. And she wanted this one, with the tiniest mole on his neck and the long, slender piano playing fingers. She only wanted this one.

She looked at him once more, this time imagining him dressed in all black – slacks, a button-up open at the neck, jacket. He would look like the clothes had been made with him in mind, cut to fit the curves of his body exclusively. The thought of how the shirt would allow glimpses of his collarbones, how it would anchor the column of his neck made her turn away in embarrassment more than his nakedness did. She wanted to see him that way, wanted to touch his neck, run her hands along those collarbones and down his back, letting her fingers dip into the gentle V that his shoulder blades created.

She needed to.

She cleared her throat.

She started.

"Spells and bells, coattails and entrails, speak ye my name in thy soul once became…"

She closed her eyes to finish the magic they had promised would work, afraid to watch, afraid to see if they had been wrong. She spoke the words she remembered and then waited. And then there was silence. Quiet—not even the sound of her breath broke through. Until…

"Your name, my elixir and for you, no more pain."

Rich.

Full-bodied.

His voice was as melodic as she had hoped it would be.

She opened her eyes to look into his attentive grays, to view his lopsided smile, lips parted to reveal perfect teeth, and said simply,

"Mine."

# THE GARAGE DOOR

THERE'S something to be said about the stamina of a 4-year-old.

People are always saying, 'I wish I could bottle some of that energy,' or some other annoying little comment that always strikes me as hollow. Those cute little one-offs always made people sound like they were just trying to find something nice to say to draw attention from the fact that the kid in question is acting like he's hopped up on something. The 'I've been where you are' comment that older ladies say to young mothers when their children run wild in the aisles of department stores, or when they eat all of the grapes before they are paid for, or, and this is priceless, when Junior decides it's time for America Idol tryouts at the deli counter, is really judgment thinly veiled as commiseration. *Tsk tsk* that seemingly understanding smile really says. *Get your shit together, Miss.* But of all the offhanded comments made by spectators of the parental variety show, that one rings true. Now, as the mother of three, shall we say, spirited children, I do want to bottle that energy. I'd sell it to folks in their fifties who are just starting to realize that the flexibility from their youth is never coming back. I'd sell it to people trying to lose weight; jumping around like the energizer bunny from sunup to sundown will surely do the trick. I'd sell it to anyone who wanted it and make a mint. Even at $1 a bottle, I'd be a millionaire within days. But one of life's cruel jokes is that you can't bottle it. You can't put it in the freezer to defrost when you really need it. All you can do it use it when you have it.

My 4-year-old understands that concept really well.

I thought maybe we could watch a little TV after music class and a play date at the park. Thought just maybe we could relax a little before naptime when I would, inevitably, fall asleep too, missing my chance to get something done. There's only a short window between having one wild thing in the house and three—just about an hour and a half. I try to vacuum, do some laundry, clean up, start dinner, and sit down for 10 minutes in that time. Sometimes I can get one or two things on the list done, but on days like today, when Mr. Baby is excited about everything he sees, I don't do anything but sleep. So I sigh, as my eyes get heavy, and settle in to a nice recline on the couch, watching Nick wind down like a top losing its juice. I didn't realize I was lying down until he climbed on top of me and got comfortable, his head on my chest, his soft hair tickling my nose. Maybe we'll just stay here on the couch for our nap instead of trudging upstairs to the bedroom. The TV's on, but that's ok. It's on a kiddie channel, so there's no chance of us waking up to a mob movie or something like that. As Nick put his arms around me, his clammy skin sticking to mine, feeling good in a way that only moms know, I decided that yeah, a nap on the sofa with my little guy would be perfect.

The sound of the garage door opening should have woken me up, but it didn't.

Oh, I heard it (its low hum is unmistakable through our

paper-thin walls), but I didn't wake up. I should have—the door opening in the middle of the day is unusual to say the least. My other two kids don't get out of school for hours, and Chris isn't due home from work until after six. More disturbing is the fact that knowing these things, I still didn't get up. Someone could be breaking in. Or what if we over-slept and the kids were opening the door with the keypad? What if someone was *making* them open the door with the keypad? For some reason, in that place between deep sleep and awake, I didn't think either of those things was happen-ing. I just figured it was Chris. He was home early, and that was all it was. Some part of my subconscious wondered why he was home early—slow day at work; playing hooky; laid off?—but didn't care enough to wake my body up to find out.

At first.

Chris took a long time getting into the house. In fact, I never heard him come inside, but I heard him moving around. That was weird because I could hear Nick's rhythmic breathing, could feel his hair under my nose if I reached for the sensation like a swimmer coasting to the surface for a breath of fresh air. But the door didn't unlock, and the alarm didn't announce his arrival with a beep. He was just there all of a sudden, puttering around in the room. I heard him drop a bag, then unzip it and rummage around inside. I heard the volume on the television turn up—one of those incessant cartoon jingles blaring suddenly, ramming the sugary-sweet lyrics about being four and, each day, growing some more down my ear canal, as if I couldn't already recite them in my sleep. I heard footsteps, Chris' socked feet approaching Nick and me on the sofa to kiss our heads like he always does when he finds us asleep on lazy weekends. I could feel myself straining towards his lips, expectantly reaching for his touch. But none came. Instead I heard raspy breathing overlaying a sickening whine—barely audible, but there, persistently there. It was so primal it affected my soul. I felt the heat from his skin as he stood over me, leaning in to peer into my face. I heard him lick his lips, his tongue flicking out like a snake's over dry lips.

That was enough to get my attention.

It wasn't that I hadn't heard ragged breath from Chris before. It had been a while, but not that long. Something about this sound, the base desperation in it, made me feel different. The usual butterflies in my stomach followed closely by warmth cascading down past my navel didn't happen. Instead I felt a sensation that I couldn't really put a finger on. Edginess? Maybe. Fear? I didn't want to admit that.

I tried to open my eyes; ready to tell him about the weirdness that started the moment he came home. He would appreciate it for what it was—an overactive imagination going full tilt. I chastised myself. It was obviously because of Nick's clammy skin and the drool that had slipped out of his mouth and onto my skin. That's why I was thinking about a wolf or a dog that we don't have, or some other panting, heavy breathing thing. He would laugh and hug me the way I like, and everything would be fine. If I'm lucky, maybe I can slip out from under Nick without waking him and have a little play date of my own. But I couldn't get my eyes to obey me. They were stuck together so well, it was as if they had been glued. I couldn't stop my mind from going to a place I had hoped I would forget. When in the dim room blanketed by humidity so stifling it was tangible and surrounded by the sickeningly sweet-smelling combination of fresh flowers and cheap perfume, I must have been the only one to see the glue giving way on Uncle Wally's eyes, the whites (well, grays considering his state of repose) winking out at me. But this time my memory of that day distorted into something far worse. Uncle Wally's right eye opened all the way, blinked, and then he turned his head toward me, his neck popping and cracking as he did it.

I tried to scream. I knew I would scare Nick and ruin any chance of having a little afternoon happy, but I needed to wake up and in a hurry. Before Uncle Wally decided to get out of the coffin and come see me. But I couldn't. I felt like my mouth was open, but there was no sound coming from my stretched vocal cords. I tried to sit up, to shake myself out of this crazy vision (oh God, why is Uncle Wally smiling?), but I couldn't move. I started to panic. I could still hear that feral breathing over me, like an animal waiting for the right time to pounce. I could see Uncle Wally lifting his head out of the coffin, his body slow to react, but moving, nonetheless. I imagined that Nick, my sweet little boy, was staring at me as I struggled, his face unreadable, impassive... cold.

I screamed.

I screamed long and loud. But that's not what I heard. The smallest, weakest crescendo emitted from my lips, building to a faint whimper, before all my limbs jumped to attention at one time. The jerk snapped me out of whatever spell I was under. It also woke Nick, my beautiful, still asleep and not staring at his mom like she was an experiment boy, up.

"Mommy! No!" He protested groggily. I kissed him on his head, the action making me acutely aware of the fact that we were alone in the room, and laid him down on the sofa. Children have an uncanny ability to fall back to sleep right away as though nothing happened. I was grateful for that today.

The room was still. I don't know why, but that made me uneasy. I mean, it should have been still if there was really only Nick and me at home, but just seconds before, I knew someone was in the room with me. Knew, not felt. And now there was no one here.

Was this a game? I almost let myself buy into that as I

stood tentatively and peered into the kitchen. Hide and seek maybe? Come find me, and quick so we can steal a couple of minutes to ourselves? I wanted to believe that. But as I saw the red Virginia clay on the floor leading from the family room—from the very sofa Nick and I were on—to the garage I knew it wasn't true.

I thought I had shut my eyes. I imagined I was standing in the family room, facing the dining room, imagined I was still waiting for Chris to pop out and whisk me to the bedroom. It was safer than where I ended up. But the door handle beneath my outstretched hand couldn't be ignored. Neither could the hot air that hit me in the face like a blast from an oven when I opened the door. I tried to shut my eyes then, tried to will away the sight of it all. But I couldn't. Partly because it didn't make sense. Chris' car would have been in the place where his shoe lay on its side. It would have filled the space where his leg bent obscenely under his body if he had come home. But he didn't come home, did he? He was still at work.

Chris' eyes were cloudy, his beautiful brown covered in a white film. That doesn't happen right away, the part of my mind that was fighting off the paralysis fear was trying to impose, rationalized. It takes at least a couple of hours for that to happen, right?

I stood there trying to figure out what I was looking at, my mind flitting back and forth between thinking it was an elaborate dream or if I was standing on some alternative plane, where reality was just a little different than the one I am from. I was in the zone; sweat coating my brow as I tried to make sense of the scene playing out in my garage, when the shuffling of feet brought me back to reality. And Chris was still there.

"Mommy, I don't wanna be 'wake," Nick said rubbing his eyes, the beginnings of a major pout sprouting on his lips. I looked at him, his hair all over his head, his eyes squinted against the light, and then back into the garage at the man I planned to spend the rest of my life with, and bit my lip. I wanted to keep biting and biting until I drew blood. Maybe that would snap me out of it. Maybe the dead Chris would disappear.

I didn't want Nick to see anything, so I closed the garage door. With any luck I could keep him away from the garage until everything was said and done and Chris had been moved.

Uncle Wally's joyless smile nagged at me.

I bit my lip a little harder than usual (just in case) and let the sob that was rushing from my throat turn into a yawn.

"Me either, baby. Me either."

# HOME PARTY

*You gotta be kidding me.*

The front of the trailer was barely visible beneath the overgrown bushes, if they could even be called bushes. They looked like the stuff that grows at the base of trees, wispy and vine-like, with pathetic little leaves that were more brown than green. Camo green. They covered the front of the trailer in clumps, like someone tried to fashion them into bushes years ago but gave up the effort and let them grow wild. Where there weren't switch-type bushes, there were bins of empty beer cans. Four of them on the splintered porch and at least three in the tall grass that made up the yard. The place stank of beer, piss, and sweat.

Carrie looked at the place, noting that two of the windows facing the front of the house were boarded up, and that the window in what might be the kitchen was so tiny, it was hard to see into. But was someone looking out? She looked around the yard. Given the state of the house, she expected there to be a bunch of discarded, rusted out cars littering the lawn, but that cliché didn't fit. There was an older model Ford, but aside from faded paint and an ancient dent on the passenger side, it had been kept up. There was a sticker in the back window from the local college. There was also a brand new pickup truck. All this was odd, but not *that* odd. They could have needed a pickup for work and maybe it isn't really new… just new to them. The Ford made total sense—a college student paying for something herself. You get what you need. That explained the beer cans too, and maybe even the boarded-up windows. One party with college kids could produce half the amount of bottles in those bins. And what's a good college party without a broken window?

But as she sat in the car, trying to rationalize everything she was seeing, she didn't believe it. The trailer didn't feel like a college hangout or a hauler's dive to crash in when he wasn't working long hours. It felt… wrong. It felt empty, but not because no one lived there. It felt lost.

Carrie swallowed, her mouth going dry while thoughts of crazy hill people of the Texas Chainsaw Massacre variety ran through her head. She forced a self-deprecating smile and got out of the car. *It's no mansion, but it's someone's house*, she told herself, and allowed for a hint of reproach to show in her inner voice. She had never been one to judge a book by its cover, as the saying goes, and she wasn't going to allow herself to start now. She straightened her smart blazer, red for the season and a perfect accompaniment to the new product line she toted with her to this afternoon's soirée. She has been excited about showing the new bags to this group of people. The lottery she posted in the local nail salon gave her entrants who wanted to have a home party and look at the new catalog items. Michele Davenport, resident at this trailer, was the lucky winner. After weeks of excited conversations, party day was here. And alone in the gravel driveway of a broken down trailer stood Carrie.

It was quiet for mid afternoon.

Carrie got back in the car, suddenly spooked. She looked at her watch. 1:30. She was supposed to get there a half an hour early, and she was late. She got stuck behind Sunday drivers on the two-lane road leading to the place and got there with only ten minutes to set up. And she ate half of that time up staring at the trailer.

Maybe there was no one there. If there was, surely they would have heard her car idling, would have seen her sitting there. As annoying as that would be (driving 45 minutes to get stood up was not her idea of a fun afternoon), Carrie didn't really want to go in the trailer. In fact, she thought, *come hell or high water, I'm not getting in the trailer.* There was something in the trailer that she didn't want to see. Something that was watching her, waiting for her to knock on the door, to look too closely at that little window in what might have been the kitchen. She could almost hear it breathing; a wet, phlegm sound that made her skin crawl. And it was watching her. It had been watching her the whole time.

Carrie turned the car on and put it in gear without looking back at that window. She didn't see the front door open, didn't see the college student's odd, slow gait toward the car. She didn't see what trailed behind her, coloring the high grass. Carrie threw her arm over the passenger seat to back out of the driveway, but a car parked her in. Laughing ladies in the front seat smiled at her, excited about the party, the games, the goodies. She didn't see the larger of the two lick her fingers as she pulled herself out of the car.

# CAUGHT

ITS BULBOUS EYE rolled its way back over to me, staring at me appraisingly, almost lasciviously. It could smell me, that much I knew; the scent of my fear was attacking my own nostrils, so I was sure it could smell me too from where it stood.

Right on the other side of the glass.

Locked between the entrance and exit—caught just like I was... almost close enough to touch.

Could they see it? The ones trying to trip the sensor, to bypass the lock and release the doors? No, they couldn't possibly. If they did, they wouldn't work so hard to get me out even if that meant they'd have to watch me die in here, the glass giving them a front row seat to my suffocation or starvation, whichever came first. No one would let something like that loose in the night, not when they couldn't be sure it wouldn't turn around and train its murderous stare on them.

Would my eyes bulge when it wrenched the life from me, wrapping its huge hands, hands as big as potato sacks—hands bigger than anything I could ever imagine—around my throat to squeeze? Would my tongue protrude? Would it stay there, distended in death to turn purple then black? Would my bowels give way, leaving a mess for the cleaning crew to deal with... my final *fuck you*?

Probably.

And wouldn't that serve them right for letting me die in here, making me pay the ultimate price for the stupidest of mistakes ever recorded? Because it was recorded, sure it was —there are cameras everywhere these days. And the guys watching the display—the two-man security faction in place during the light foot traffic hours sitting in a room the size of a closet and watching shitty black and white monitors rippling with interference every few seconds—probably laughed their asses off while I, lost in thought, walked in a circle, following the door as it crawled, spinning slowly enough to go gray waiting for it to come back around. I ignored the exit not once or twice, but four times only to find myself locked in the revolving door of an aging hotel, one that had sprung for motion sensors but had neglected to actually put one *inside* the contraption. What was on my mind that was so important escapes me now as I listen to the obscene licking of lips, spitty and wet, and hear the hiss and sizzle as saliva falls to the floor, burning it like acid—something about changing my clothes before the night's festivities, or—no, it wasn't just that. That's not enough to make you walk around in a circle, passing go but saying screw your rightfully earned $200...

I know full well what I was thinking about and maybe, just maybe, I deserve this shit because of it.

The men outside the revolving door had brought out the power tools now.

Someone had the company that manufactured the death-trap on the phone, but at this hour—pre-witching hour, but dead of night still the same—they were likely talking to the poor sap saddled with overnights... the one who hadn't needed to handle a trouble call in years.

That bulbous eye is looking at me again, sending the visual to its brain to devour.

I stare back, unable to look away though my mind begs me to, trying to chant it out of existence even as its saliva burns through the metal at the bottom of the door.

# SENSORY BOWL

"Eggs," Darryl said matter-of-factly, like he knew everything about everything. "They use eggs for the eyeballs."

"No, they don't," Sherry said, coming back just as confidently and with a hint of irritation that would grow sharper when she moved into her teenage years, morphing into a kind of condescension that could bring a man to his knees. "They use mozzarella for that. The fresh kind. You know, the stuff that comes packed in water?"

Darryl *didn't* know—that much was clear by just looking at his face—but he wasn't willing to admit it out loud. I didn't know either, couldn't even call the memory of seeing cheese in water before, let alone how they could use it for eyeballs. I mean, what? Did they take the slices and roll them into balls or something?

"No, they don't," Darryl said, but when he said it, he sounded like every bit the twelve-year-old he was, obstinate and adolescent. Not like Sherry, who sounded mature and smart. Not like Sherry, who was twelve just like they were, even a few months younger than they were, but seemed three years older, seemed like she was already a teenager, looked like she was already a teenager.

"Are you serious?" Sherry said, a laugh playing on her lips, lips with sparkly lip gloss on them, the one she always put on after she left the house and rounded the corner out of her mother's sight, like now. I didn't get why she hid it—it wasn't like it was lipstick or anything. It wasn't even red. But then I remembered that one day when her mom saw her with it on, called her back to the house, and made her wipe it off. I remember that I looked at Darryl to see if he was hearing what I was hearing. Sherry's mom was yelling at her about it, saying she wasn't allowed to wear it, said she *knew* she wasn't, and how disappointed she was that Sherry had put it on. When she came out, Sherry was embarrassed, but we didn't say anything.

I guess whatever happened between her and her mother didn't matter, though, because her lips were glistening again, catching the light and reflecting it back to me like the stars in the night sky.

"—right, Chef? I mean, I know *you* know."

Know... what?

Know *what*!?

I don't know what she's talking about, wasn't listening to them, not really—at least not right then. I had been looking at them, sure, at least... ok, I had been looking at her, watching her glossy lips as they formed the words, as they formed my name—well, not really my name, but what they called me all the time. Chef. It's stupid, really—the reason they call me Chef. One day after school, they came over to my house because both of their parents had to work late. My mom got pulled into a conference call right before we walked in the door so she hadn't made the snack she had planned to, so I made something instead. It was nothing—just cinnamon sugar chips. Literally four ingredients—cinnamon, sugar, butter, and flour tortillas—but because I knew how to cut them into perfect wedges and how long to cook them in the oven, I would forever be known as Chef. And maybe it stuck because me and my dad watch *MasterChef* every week, and I mean, ok, maybe I have been not-so-secretly hoping for a revival of *Turn Up the Heat* with G. Garvin.

Chef.

Whatever.

"Chef knows, he's just trying not to make you feel stupid out here in these streets," Sherry continued in my silence, mercifully filling the space with her words like she knew I needed her to take the spotlight off me, like she knew I needed her help. She never says my name anymore, I realized. Neither one of them did. They were my best friends in the whole world, and neither of them called me by the name my parents chose for me, the name that I actually really like. Kyle. I don't know any other Kyles, so I feel unique, special.

Kyle Spencer.

An entertainer's name. Maybe an actor's name. Not a football or basketball player—that'll never be me—but it's still a name that might be up in lights one day.

Maybe I'll be on TV.

Maybe I'll have my own *cooking show* on TV…

"-—have to fold you—"

"What?!?"

I spoke before I realized I had planned to, said it louder than I had ever intended to. But if Darryl had been stupid enough to threaten Sherry, well, I wasn't just going to stand by and let that happen. We were best friends. She was, I mean she was *Sherry*. Silly, opinionated, pretty—

Wait, wh—

Darryl was laughing.

Sherry was laughing.

Darryl and Sherry were laughing.

Together.

Hands on shoulders, hands over mouths, hands covering stomachs, and resting on top of knees as they bowled over, laughter shaking their bodies.

"You—you should see your face," Darryl said between breaths snatched before laughter took over again.

"It was like you woke up from one of those dreams, the ones where you can't move and you're all freaked out and you start yelling—"

"Sleep paralysis," Sherry supplied, tears coming to her eyes as she tried to quell her laughter. "Only you were awake. It was crazy."

Laughing. Not fighting. Darryl hadn't been stupid enough to try to hit Sherry. Come to think of it, the voice talking about folding was too high to have been Darryl's in the first place. Too high and too melodic, sweet, lyrical. And totally facetious. Threats of folding people came out of their mouths all the time. The reason why didn't really matter—it was almost like a way to end a disagreement—a closing sentence in a conclusion paragraph. None of them had ever hit the other, unless you called fouls on the court hits. And they never would. They were friends. Friends who had grown up together, respected each other, loved each—

Wait…

"You good, bro?" Darryl said, finally straightening up, his laughter trickling down to a chuckle at the back of his throat.

"Yeah, you ok?" Sherri said, only I heard something different. They weren't words, really, at least not ones that I could pick out. But she sang them, and they danced in the air between us. She sang them, and the breath she used to form them tickled my nose.

No, I'm not ok.

No, I'm not good.

"Yeah," I said instead, getting hold of myself just before my mind betrayed me and professed my undying love to the girl I had known since I was in diapers. Because it *is* love. I know that now. And I am so very screwed.

"W—what are you gonna be?" I said, tearing my eyes away from hers, addressing no one in particular but really, really, really anxious to hear what she was going to say.

"I don't even know," Darryl said, speaking first. He said he didn't know, but he did. He had been planning his costume for longer than he would willingly admit.

"Last one," Sherry said, and a kind of melancholy descended on us, slumping our shoulders a bit, slowing our steps. It hung in the air in front of us, that comment, what it meant. Last one. Last Halloween before we might be too old to show that we cared about Halloween. The last Halloween where we could trick or treat without feeling silly, like little kids. Last one before we became TEENAGERS and started driving and having sex and smoking pot and going to college and getting real jobs.

It was the last one.

"I'm going as The Joker. The new one from the movie," I said, my voice sounding far away in my head.

"You didn't even see the movie," Sherry said, her voice dripping with incredulousness that I might come to hate at some point but right now I loved every bit of it. And yeah, she was right. I hadn't seen the movie. My mom said it was dark, said it was complex and more adult than it should be considering it was about a comic book character. Sherry knew I hadn't seen it because her mom and my mom were besties. Same with Darryl's mom. The three of them met in a Moms club when we were just about a year old—just starting to crawl and knock things over at the playdates they had twice a week. We've done it all together—started school, gone to camp, watched our first scary movie, gone on vacation. And it was good—always good, except we had no secrets. If one of us didn't tell the other about something, our parents told each other and somehow the information got to us. I knew Darryl was afraid of Ben Grimm before he told me because his mother and mine were looking him up in our kitchen one day, trying to figure out what the big deal was. My mom got mad at me when I turned on the Fantastic Four when Darryl was over later that week and even though I tried to play it off like I didn't remember, she knew. Whatever. Darryl kept blocking my shot on the court at recess— had been doing it for a whole month before I decided to make him squirm. Basketball star I am not, but I didn't need my boy showing me up like that. He deserved to piss his pants a little.

"You didn't see *Hellraiser,* but that doesn't stop you from being a pinhead," Darryl said, and I laughed in spite of myself. Because it was right on time. And funny as hell.

Sherry screwed up her face at him and then at me when my laughter broke free from my throat and shot into the air. She hit me then, like she always did when a burn was actually funny but she didn't want to admit it. She hit Darryl too, but I didn't see it. I was too busy feeling the place on my arm where she had struck me tingle, grow warm like it was under a laser. I rubbed it, then covered it with the palm of my hand as if to protect it from the elements. If I didn't think they would notice and call me as sus for it, I would have brought my hand to my lips and kissed it.

"Your mom's going all out for this one," Sherry said, moving on gracefully.

"Yeah, 'cause it really is the last one. The last Halloween party—at least the last one she's gonna throw. She said that when I turn 13, I'm gonna want to go to somebody else's party, do things outside the house."

"She's kinda right," Darryl said, but there was a hint of

sadness to it. The Halloween party had been an event we had looked forward to for years. Our house had been the place to be on Halloween since we were babies. We would party together, go trick or treating together, and then come back and watch a scary movie. We graduated from Scooby-Doo to *Goosebumps* in my living room wearing sweaty costumes and stuffing our mouths with candy.

We fell silent, walking at the same pace that we always did, first me, then Sherry, then Darryl in a row. I know what they were thinking, just like they knew what was in my head: everything was about to change. You could almost smell it in the air—there was just no escaping it. And even if we railed against our parents when they didn't let us have take-out when we want or caught attitudes when they asked us if we had homework even though we did, some part of us wasn't ready to let go of candy apples, not-so-scary movies, and freeze dance competitions to "Monster Mash". It was embarrassing, all the decorations and the activity stations our parents set up for face painting, pin the tail on the donkey, and find the creepy crawlies. Sometimes I cringe when I think about what my friends—the ones from school—will think when my dad wins the annual "Thriller" dance competition again, like he does every year because he grew up mimicking Michael Jackson, and he is all too eager to pull out those dance moves even if he has to do so in a ghoul costume. The corny maze in the backyard, the pumpkin stab, the candy sort—it was all kid stuff, but what we weren't saying out loud, what was taking over our minds as we walked to Ms. Elianna's house was that we *wanted* to sit in the middle of the floor sorting our candy while *Goosebumps* played in the background and my dad caught his breath on the sofa. We wanted that because it was as much a part of us as anything else and not having it made us wonder who we were.

"Why'd she make us come all the way over here to get a cauldron? You can get one of those from the store," Sherry asked as we approached the house.

"She said something about art too, something else we're supposed to pick up." We slowed to a stop as if in lockstep, finding ourselves in front of Ms. Elianna's house before we realized it. I didn't know who Ms. Elianna was—none of us did—but we were in front of her house anyway, picking up stuff Mom bought for the Halloween party on the online community garage sale. Stuff for the *last* party.

Ugh.

"Art? How are we gonna get that home?" Darryl asked a little too loudly.

"It can't be that big. She wouldn't have sent us if it was. And it's not like we have to walk a mile—we're like two streets away from the house."

My house, Sherry's house, Darryl's house—all of them were 'the house' because each of them felt just like home.

"Man..."

"Shut up, dude. It's for the party."

Darryl and I cut across the grass but Sherry used the path, making me feel both childish and disrespectful instantly. I wouldn't meet Sherry's eyes, but I could feel them on my face, just knew she was making a face that screamed her disapproval, lips screwed up into some kind of half grimace/ half smile that I didn't fully understand but didn't like the look of anyway.

"That's what's up," I said because I felt like I needed to say something. I pointed my chin in the direction of Ms. Elianna's door and the wreath that hung on it. It reminded me of something I saw on a bumper sticker that said COEXIST in all these symbols I didn't recognize, well, except the peace sign, the yin and yang, and the cross for the 'T'. Mom said it was supposed to show that there's space for everyone. I just liked the way it looked.

The wreath on Ms. Elianna's door kind of looked like the one the sticker used for the 'X' but with more peaks and loops. I found myself trying to follow the loops as they wove around the straight lines that formed points and would have kept doing it even though the sounds of the streets—the birds chirping, gears shifting as cars started up the hill ahead —were fading away, if Sherry hadn't snapped me out of my reverie.

"What?"

"That wreath."

She didn't respond. I was surprised how irritated I was to have to look away from the wreath to see why.

Her face as screwed up again. I was noticing a pattern.

"Hmph."

Lips curled into a side pucker. Hand on her hip.

"What?"

Same face, some posture. I felt the back of my neck getting hot.

"No cap. I like it," I said, and I meant every word.

Sherry rolled her eyes and looked away from me, turning her attention to the wreath. I wanted to tell her not to look at it with that smirk on her face, wanted to warn her that it might not like it.

"I bet your mom is gonna use the cherry pie filling for the blood this time," Darryl said as he mounted the steps toward the front door, oblivious of the exchange between Sherry and me. "It'll be thick and nasty, like congealing blood."

"Ooh, and gummy worms and licorice laces for muscles and tendons," Sherry chimed in, a light switch shutting off whatever unpleasantness existed before.

"Maybe rock candy for brittle bones. She'll mix it all up in the bowl." Darryl actually sounded excited.

It was contagious.

"And don't forget gummy tarant—-," I started but then the door opened without us knocking, and a woman who looked like she was 200 years old stood in the doorway. We had to look down to see her; the bend in her back was that deep. When she spoke, it was no louder than a whisper and Darryl leaned toward her to hear, using his polite voice to ask her to repeat herself, and I wish he hadn't. I wish Darryl hadn't stepped inside to see whatever she was gesturing towards. I wish Sherry hadn't followed, smiling at the old woman and saying she would help Darryl. I wish we were kids again and the last Halloween party was a long way off, so far off that my mom hadn't thought about a way to make this party the best one ever, hadn't tried to give it a big sendoff. I wish I could have passed out before thinking about

Eggs.

Darryl had said they used eggs for the eyeballs in the sensory bowl, but he had been wrong. So had Sherry when she said they used fresh mozzarella. They'd never guess what was really in the bowl... never.

# GOODBYE

HE HEARD their footsteps more clearly now; they were right above of him, racing around the top floor in search of the scent that tantalized their nostrils and fueled the pit of desire sitting heavy in their stomachs. They were in search of food, in search of blood. He gathered his papers, documents that would mean nothing if he didn't get out of his sister's renovated home, perpetually under construction. It was a place she had put so much time and work into—a place she would never see finished. He tossed the papers into the tattered duffle bag that sat by the front door and forced the zipper over them and what clothing he could gather before they broke the upstairs window and came inside. They would find enough to occupy themselves upstairs, at least for a few minutes; his niece, his precious Julia, wasn't quite in the throes of death when he'd left her in her bed, knowing it would be the last time he laid eyes on her. Surely, she hadn't died yet. If she had, there would be no hope for escape.

With a fleeting glimpse around the house, his eyes falling on antiques his sister had combed Paris for, their grandmother's rocking chair, his sister's lifeless eyes staring at him from the sofa where she had succumbed, he said goodbye to everyone he held dear. Staying to pick up something—anything—to remember them by would mean certain death. He knew that, logically, but still he eyed the picture of his family on the table next to the sofa. It had fallen over onto its side, knocked there when his sister had stumbled into the room, taking her last steps. He wanted to take the picture with him, to walk the five steps between the foyer and living room and snatch it from the side table, but he couldn't. Walking into the living room would leave him vulnerable to spying eyes on the top floor. As it was, they might be able to see his shadow along the wall from where he stood.

They could be looking at him right now.

Either way, it wouldn't be long before they would know there was someone else in the house. They would smell his blood like they smelled Julia's.

He had to go.

His life depended on it.

The closing door almost spared him the muted shriek escaping Julia's dying lips.

# NEXT

---

Loud.

So loud when he left, the door slamming behind him, echoing throughout the room, bouncing from one side to the other of my head, my brain, my soul.

Gone.

Gone because his job is done.

It is over for him, and he can leave, can run, can distance himself from this forever if he chooses to, really.

But for me, it has just begun.

She looks so pretty there, with her hair haloing her head, brown and thick, curly, glossy.

Healthy.

Liar.

He left without saying anything, nothing at all, actually, not even as she spoke her frustrations, choosing then, then, even then to tell him how she felt. How he failed her. How beneath her he was.

How base.

Fine.

That was her choice.

But didn't he know that I was here? Sure, he did—he saw me at her hem, small there where I had never been small before. He saw me, yet he still left and that, well, that is fine. It has to be. What else can it be now?

The door boomed when he left. Could she hear it where she was?

Where is she?

What is she now that all of this is said and her armor has been laid down, battlement left unguarded?

What am I?

White and gold.

And red.

Her velvet, saturated through, dark red against the wine.

Makes brown.

Like a stain.

Gold bangles to accent skin that won't be the same tomorrow, today, ever again.

He left me there to watch still set and gray color with the hope that osmosis, proximity, divine clarity showed itself between these gilded walls.

Coward.

Bring forth the bejeweled cup and drinketh yourself, you bastard.

Perhaps she had been right about him all along.

Her hair is splayed so beautifully on the floor. Gold and purple hair tinsel thin as filament threaded through, spiraling delicately among the strands: the identity of the royal. So like my own but more in every way... more prevalent, more vibrant, more deserved. I touch my own strands, find the tinsel and pull but it doesn't come, honey's paste secure and the practitioner talented as they are expected to be considering the coif upon which they work.

My ringed fingers twitch, unsure what to touch next.

The eyes of the seer to see.

The tongue of the speaker to speak.

Pray tell which first? Which not at all?

Legs cramped beneath my frock but still I sit as I am destined to do. My place here is written, and I shall not move unless struck down.

But for how long?

How long am I to sit here as I fell, not moving a muscle, feeling my limbs turn to stone, grow cold as the floor, cold as rock, cold as she?

How long?

The books were never read, my lady, the rules never navigated. When does the sexton mark the death knell?

Cold.

Chill in the air from the window open to the world. Cold outside as it is within. Even Mother Nature bends to her will.

Silent.

Quiet as death.

Death outside.

Death inside.

Blood on the ground.

Blood on the floor.

Seeping, pooling, sinking, congealing, permeating, invading, red, red, red death the final and I see, I see I see it from here I see it, I tell you, I see it all.

Sight to blind me.

Sight to school me.

Predator, you fiend, I know you well.

Spare one or none, I no longer care because the tinsel in her hair stays firm even when they would rot out before long, rot out by the heat of the sun. Rot out because rot it must as she no longer is.

But then who is next?

He left because he was supposed to. Prince that he was, from family outside of the province. Never given proper title and oh, did it anger him. 'Twas girl that was born and only one such that he could not kill to take the throne. Ah yes, he left because he cannot stay. And that is fine as well.

I shed my rings. They are of no use to me now.

Imperial Topaz cut in the shape of her mother's tears sitting in the finest Indian gold. Too big for my finger, but I feel it grip me as it slides easily down, slick with blood.

And I sit.

The hills beyond are green in the spring when life buds new all over the land. I see them now, and though they should be covered with grass and flowers that I might pick and bring home for her to smell, to see, to love, they are brown to my veiled eyes. Though life abounds there, I see death, can feel the soil littered with bodies and choking on the blood that waters it relentlessly, forcing it to drink, to fill to the brim, to die along with the one that cultivated it. Go on, then. Die as you might, fickle grass. I shall never see your beauty again, not even the innocence of a tulip will sway my eye. Should I ever get up to see you clearly again, that is. Therefore, it matters not if you die or do not.

Mouth open.

My mouth is open.

Her mouth is open.

Breath tickles my nose.

What comes from the open mouth when the speaker has lost their voice?

Over that hill is the town named for her father's father, or so the story goes. He was beloved there, was a soldier that had saved the town from conquer. In his honor they named it so to remember him by, painted his likeness, and put it on the map.

People care about us, she said.

Then where are they?

I sit.

I wait.

The sun dips behind the hill that marks my territory, and I wait.

Where are these people that care for us so much? Where is the one who should be here to decide what comes next but cannot?

*The queen is silenced*, I want to yell but know that I should not, because it isn't true, is it?

No, the queen is not silenced, is she? Because she…

The people of old made it so that people could eat, she used to say. Right over that hill stood tall buildings, bridges, and motorized cars. They went to work every day, buying and selling, creating and testing, giving and taking. They had more money than they knew what to do with and spent it all, letting it flow from their hands, their pockets, their bank accounts, like water running from a tap, greed the font. They laughed gaily throughout the night and woke up ill but did it all over again at every week's end. There was theater, and there was shopping, and there were sporting events to rival our own. The rich were so very rich and the poor, in some places, still had enough to fund an existence for the down-trodden our rule were accustomed to. But then he died, and the world stopped.

It froze.

It waited.

It waited for someone to say something, do something. Take over. Take charge. Take initiative.

But the ones who would do so were dead, and the town sank to its knees.

Money burned.

Towers burned.

People burned.

My family left.

Came over the hill and fortified the land to protect them from anyone else who would do so after them.

They waited.

They watched.

The shots in the night used to be numerous, Mother said. And this is what her mother had told her when she was a child. But by the time my mother was old enough to listen for them herself, they were gone. The sounds of the night, the low, wailing hum that accompanied every moment of every day in their beautiful valley, the only sound that was ever heard. And you never heard it, not really. Because it was always there, it was part of the background as much as the zebras that graze in the fields were.

Until it was gone.

Then all you could hear was the absence of it.

Nothingness.

What's over the hill now, Mama?

What do you see, Mama?

Nothing.

Corset too tight.

Mine or hers to loosen first?

Ankle twisted beneath her as she fell, broken bone pressing against skin.

Black and blue.

Bruised when blood flowed.

My ankle aches, bent awkwardly beneath heavy, motionless girth.

Must I mirror or can I move to prevent the ruin, Mama?

Must I be…

… Mama?!?

Flies buzzing overhead.

Flies with little legs that land on anything, everything. Legs with spiked hairs on them, barbed hairs that catch bits and pieces of whatever they landed on and take it with them. Pollen, dander, feces. Carried to and fro, clinging to them as the flies buzzed overhead looking for something new to land on.

I hate flies.

I hate bugs.

I hate their very nature to invade personal space, claiming everything in the world for their own if only for a second, a moment in time. Nasty, dirty, despicable things that carry disease, germs, the blood of enemies, the blood of...

Buzz.

Buzz.

Buzz.

Lands.

Lands on her face.

Rubs its legs together while sitting on her cheek.

Walks into her eye.

I want to swat it way.

Shouldn't I swat it away?

Did she swat away the flies that landed in her mother's eyes? Her father's?

Laying eggs.

I am sure the fly is laying eggs in her eye, and they will fester there, safe, warm, and protected until they hatch. And they'll hatch before the pyre, won't they? Hatch just before she is placed upon it so that all can see the movement beneath the sheet, so that all can imagine them crawling , wriggling free, stretching their newfound wings, rubbing their feet together to rid them of her viscosity.

Twelve hours... maybe 24.

Soon.

She told me of the day her mother was stung by a bee. How she passed out when they took out the stinger and didn't wake up for days, months, years. I was six then and had just swatted a bee when my mother told me that, and I cried and cried, afraid the bee and his whole bee family would come after me for all my days, never letting me rest until they had all stung me to sleep.

Twelve bees… maybe 24.

Life.

Death.

She doesn't blink when the fly dances on her eye, so I blink for her.

She told me I would one day wear the finest silks and lace. I would trot out a handsome man to take as my partner while I sat on the throne. She said I would be ready for love but not ready to lead when my time came, but that it wouldn't matter. I answered no, that time would never come because men were all bores, especially the pretty ones. And as for leading, well on that account she was right. I would bid her goodnight if only to play along with her rhyme. But she always *tsked tsked* me as I spoke and told me she knew more than I did.

Indeed.

I am not ready.

Not ready for love nor ready to lead.

There is no handsome man to stand by the side of my throne. My intended has no interest in the trivialities of the throne. He would rather hunt and gather, go over the hill and make money to bring back to his garden to bury at night. My intended does not know he is my intended at all. He does not know how I watch him as he goes in his travels, reading his commentary of the world so close but yet so far.

Parasocial.

Paranormal.

Parasomnia.

I talk to him while I'm asleep.

He looks like he hears because he smiles and laughs, and oh, when he smiles I can't help but smile too because she had it right on that score, she knew what she was talking about when she said he'd be that, for sure.

Pretty.

So very pretty.

And when he smiles he lights up the room, and his eyes squint, and his face glows.

Eye candy.

And when he laughs he can't breathe, and his body leans to the side, and you hold your breath because all you want to do is laugh too, but you don't know if you should because he doesn't know you, doesn't see you, doesn't hear you, doesn't get you, but oh, he is laughing again, and I can't stop watching.

He likes blue, and I like him so I watch him laugh and chuckle along quietly alongside him from across the king-dom, wondering if he notices. Lots of girls choose him, but he will choose me because I am perfect for him because he is perfect to me.

He is so pretty when he smiles.

My giggle is so loud it is deafening but so quiet I wonder if he can hear.

He will stand beside me as I sit on the throne that is mine, mine, rightfully mine. And he will smile so pretty, and the kingdom will adore him because he looks like he should be adored, and they will throw flowers at his feet, and he will give them all to me because it is me that he serves and will serve forever.

Can you see him, Mama?

Can you see me and him?

I will leave the castle and live by the beach because I love the water and that is where I want to be. The kingdom will be there, and they will throw rose petals at my feet as I walk along the sand. I will kick at the water, and it will tickle my toes in retribution because it loves me and I love it and it is mine and mine alone. And that is how I will spend my days, kicking at the water and watching movies in the sky.

Tell me, Mama, tell me what I am to do now that a skin has formed on your blood as it grows cold there on the white, staining the white, marring it forever and always?

Do I cast out those who would not fight for me?

Do I make my first decree, say something pertinent, something important, something you would never say but that you have already said long ago when you were young and it didn't matter?

Do I call for my love to be by my side because he is mine and not hers, mine and always has been, mine forever?

Perhaps.

But after.

Once my legs no longer feel attached to my body and they are as cold as ice.

Once the sun dips down past the hill and the lights turn on on the other side to glow in the sky.

Once the fly is done playing in your eye and leaves to light on something else.

I once impaled a moth on a toothpick.

I watched it as it wriggled, the throes of death short and sweet.

I showed the toothpick to my mother as she was the only one I thought would look at it and truly see the beauty. She said I should not make it suffer so unless the other moths saw and understood.

Did the moths see and understand? Should I open the chamber and let them pass, giving the queen a wide berth as they looked on, the message hanging before them like a neon sign

What was the message?

For whom was it written?

I will trail my finger in her blood later and scribe along the white to make matters clear.

I will write it on my body so that I remember too.

War paint.

Tribal markings engraved deep in the skin, deep in the soul.

Contouring.

Mask donned, removable not removed.

She told me once about a tattoo she had that no one knew about. A small thing that looked like a blemish to anyone who might get close enough to see it.

I want to see it.

I want to see it now.

The queen is dead, and I want to see it.

I am the queen, and I want to see it.

I think I shall get one of my own once I know who I am.

I think I shall hide it in the manner of a queen.

My decree: all queens shall get a tattoo that they hide for the rest of their days.

Is that good enough, Mama?

He is back, but I want him to leave.

He is here to light the torches, but I want the darkness.

The white glows against it like a fluorescent. The red is as black as tar.

"Go," I tell him, "for I have not learned all yet. There is more she can give me."

I can feel his concern from here, but I do not move. I do not turn my head. I do not shift.

He does not come closer.

The blood has long ago been cut off from my leg.

Numb feels like something.

Numb feels like nothing.

Nothing hurts.

She told me once to stop doing something if it hurt, but I

didn't listen. I did it anyway. I flapped my hand back and forth until my wrist felt it might break; I forced my legs into a split when they didn't want to go.

I stared at the sun even though she told me not to.

It showed me black dots.

It showed me death.

Her blood on white, black as midnight.

My blood.

"Do you see?" I asked the unfortunate who was volunteered to stick her head in and look upon us. "She lies so peacefully."

The woman wants to say something but knows she shouldn't. I could have her tongue if she spoke words I found distasteful. Mother would not have liked that. Mother would not have done that, but I am not mother, cannot be mother, will never be mama. And so she is silent because she knows what is good for her.

Be kind and rewind.

Her mother played hopscotch with mine as children. She thinks that matters to me.

And it does.

If you do the crime, you do the time.

They played hand clapping games on park benches, thick paint, soft from so many coats, covering splintered wood.

> *Miss Mary Mack Mack Mack*
> *all dressed in black black black*
> *with silver buttons buttons buttons*
> *all down her back back back*

She thinks that matters to me.
And it does.
Mama smiled when I missed.
I smiled too.

Maybe we will go over the hill together, my pretty thing and me. Maybe he will put me on his back and carry me over it, and we'll never come back.

Maybe she was the last queen.

Maybe the queen has decided to call it done.

But then where would they get their grain? Their hay? Their wood?

Where would they sing their songs or drink ale as they pleased after a long day in the fields?

What would they do?

What if everyone over here followed me over there, crowding in, dimming the beautiful lights that light up the sky with their numbers?

What would she think when the kingdom was chewed up and spit out?

My hair would be long and straight, pink and purple and turquoise and blue.

I would have lost the gold, it wouldn't have mattered anymore.

And what of it?

What could she do?

She couldn't reprimand me, send me to my room, banish me to the badlands, make me live with the crows. She couldn't ground me, take my access, forbid me to watch my pretty as he goes to the restaurants, the movies, the park making everyone turn their heads, smile at him and hope he deigns to return it. I'd still see him because he'd be on the other side of the hill in my hand, rubbing shoulders with those who walk the side-walks and wear sundresses and shorts. He'd be there with lights illuminating his face while glasses clanked and silverware clinked against plates. I could speak to him while he ate, his bite my bite because he made it so, showing me everything because he knows I would love it as much as he does. She couldn't stop me even if she could try.

But she can't.

Try.

She couldn't do any of that because the red is on the white, and it is black like the night.

She can't even swat the fly away from her eyes.

One hundred billion stars and she sees every one of them.

Tell me, do they gleam? Do they shimmer, mama? Or are they muted and cold, burnt out?

Do I want to know?

Shadows crawl across the floor, and I hear my breath retreat into my mouth. A new day is dawning outside, and the people over the hill are waking, stretching, yawning.

The house is awake because the queen is awake.

I sit looking at the ring... her ring... my ring and know that my leg will work when I move it from under my body, heavy with responsibility. I know that she has told me everything I needed to know and that I have heard it all.

I know that she is dead.

He comes to the room tentatively again, footsteps outside the door pacing, waiting, milling until I bid him enter. He looks tired, and I know that he will step back. I know that he wants to step back. Leading had never been the thing that he wanted. He had been her handsome man standing next to her while she sat on her throne. And now that she was dead, he would be happy to let the next man come in to perform the duty that was no longer his. And that was fine.

"I rise, father," I say but he doesn't hear me. I move to stand but my legs don't obey. I look at the sky and notice the clouds forming. The pyre will be pretty on this gray day.

"What you want you already have, child," he says without saying it, eyes cascading over me again as they had yesterday.

He does not look at her.

He does not see what I saw move under my gaze.

He does not see…

He leaves again, a heavy sigh causing him to shiver as he walks away from her, away from me… away.

Perhaps, dear father, you were right after all.

Daylight comes, and I can no longer bear to look at her.

She told me this moment would come and here it is. But I cry anyway because I can feel the door closing, the page turning. I can feel my growing pains as she told me I used to as a child, can feel myself growing larger even as she grows smaller, her light extinguished and body changed. And it hurts, and it is real, and I cry. I cry for myself. I cry for her. I cry for the queen.

I hope it pleases her that I now know the steps are my own, just as it was for hers. Her journey was unique as mine will be, and my beginning was epic and noteworthy in its silence, in its bloody residue. As I come out on the other side of the night that was to be the last as I knew it with the common eyes I was so desperate to keep, clarity has been granted. She could no more have helped me than I will help mine when the time comes.

She told me once that I was formidable, and I believe that now. She said I could withstand anything, even the horror of night, and she was right. The red on white is proof of that.

I draw my sword and don't hesitate to make the cut that is required, the cut that is expected. My palm bleeds freely, and that is fine, coating her hand and drenching the floor, my blood mingling with hers spilled so many hours before.

Rusty, oxidized topped with the fresh red of life.

Out with the old and in with the new.

I stand, and it hurts but that is fine. I look at the ring that is now mine, the one that fits me perfectly the way no other has before and know what needs to be done. Movement catches the corner of my eye as it had a moment ago, as it had an hour before.

White.

Small.

Like a grain of rice.

A nothing.

But it is everything in a wink.

The pyre will cleanse it all.

The fire will get them before they get her.

Long live the queen.

# COMING

THEY CAME IN THE DARK.

Like a mob, they gathered together in motion, moving as one, advancing, coming, coming.

The streetlamp illuminated the face of a neighbor who drank his beer on his front steps and exchanged pleasantries the other day.

A wayward flashlight beam revealed the face of the cashier at the supermarket around the corner.

With guns and bats and chains and knives they came, sure and steady, enjoying the press, the terror, the fear.

Silence from one direction, loud music from the other, rhythmic bass thumping and electric guitar squealing cutting through the silence, warring with each other outside in the dark... deep down beneath the skin.

Voices rising, wrestling for control, out of sync in the din but the message so very clear.

*Bang!*

The cross was hammered home in the soft grass, on the sterile wall, on the casket lid.

*Bang!*

The door shook on its hinges, sound erupting in the dead of night.

*Bang!*

The blood, deafening as it rushed to the head, pressing, beating, pleading.

*Bang!*

White looks gray against an overcast sky.

*Bang!*

Branches snap beneath weight they were never meant to hold.

*Bang!*

Cellphones flash, snapping pictures that will shape history but be too late for security.

Is the lamb's blood painted above the door?

Are the papers in order?

*Bang…*

# ICE CREAM

How does it feel?

She had watched as it happened, saw the color drain from his eyes as his capillaries burst and his skin seemed to rip apart, to disintegrate, the destruction brought by something inside... something that wanted, demanded, required center stage.

Did it hurt, that usurping, that overtaking?

Did it... hurt?

She had watched him go through the stages like she was watching a movie on the silver screen. It was method acting at its finest—a real display of talent if ever there was one, 'Man Afraid to Die' the prompt. He got angry, thrashed as he felt the teeth rip into him, pulling at his flesh to take some away. He screamed in anger as he cut down the one that cost him his life, releasing all that welled up from his stomach to his chest, up his throat to spill out of his mouth in loud, foul torrents. The anger gave way to sobs which brought on tears that hadn't stopped until he breathed his last. He was sad that he was dying, sorry he had hesitated, had turned the wrong corner, had ever moved to the state, wished he'd never bought her an ice cream by the lake... never told her he loved her. He regretted every perceived misstep—wished he'd never laid eyes on her at all, but he had... he had, and his only solace, as his mind fractured under the weight of true under-standing of his fate and the poison actively taking root, was that he had exacted revenge. He mourned every decision that he had ever made that brought him to that place, the ones that condemned him, damned him in those final moments.

And then he felt the pain.

But what was it like? The pain... was it searing, like a fire burning the layers of skin one by one, making its way down to the nerves, driving him mad with the relentless heat? Was it cold like winter, numbing and sharp like the tip of an icicle as it pierced the flesh? Did he want to rub at it—the place where he had been bitten—did he want to pull at it, squeeze it the way one might a pimple, rip out the bad?

Did he feel the powder on the back of his tongue, residue from his grinding teeth protesting the loss, the fast-approaching rot? Was it bitter?

Did he feel hot?

Was he sweating? Or was he parched and dry?

Did he smell something sweet?

Did his feet and hands tingle with anticipation? Could he feel his blood slowing in his veins? Could he smell himself, the fecal matter he had prematurely released, the pungent muskiness that was nearly intolerable to breath in?

What was it *like*?

She had asked him. Over and over as she watched the cone—double chocolate and peanut butter fudge—melt on the sidewalk, discarded, forgotten. She had begged him at the end, seeing his eyes cloud over, knowing she was losing her chance to find out.

Drip.

Drip.

Drip.

But he never spoke. The bastard. He never said a thing… at least not when she could hear him over her own screams.

# DISC GOLF

It wasn't the red that distracted them, though that would easily have been enough.

Growing there, one small tuft with seeds on the tips, wispy like wheat, waiting for the wind to carry them away so they could take root somewhere else, plant themselves, infest the ground... it looked out of place. It *was* out of place. The place is its now. And even the animals knew it.

Alone.

Left alone to flourish.

To multiply.

But no. It remained small, compact, red blades against the most brilliant green Lori had ever seen. Emerald and basil and pear infected by some poison, some other, some parasitic more.

Red.

Lori opened her mouth to call Kelsey over to see it, but then closed it without making a sound. Because she was already seeing it. They all had to be—the red was almost glowing in the shaded wood, the canopy of leaves above them trapping the light and muting everything else.

Millie had found the car, some rusted out 1950s vintage model that Lori's boyfriend Steve would have flipped over had he come along. But he hadn't come along, and maybe that was good, she found herself thinking. Maybe that was better.

*Steve wouldn't have known what it was either. But he would have texted Matt, and he would have looked it up. He would have tried to find out. He would have gotten help. He would have—*

*Steve would have touched it.*

*What would have happened if Steve had touched it?*

A gasp.

Billie?

Millie?

Kelsey?

It was loud enough to snap Lori out of her head. Brought her back to the present just in time to pull her outstretched hand away from the red.

Kelsey was looking at a pick-up truck nearby. It looked like it was part of the hill, dirt and moss, grass and roots pulling it in to something that could only be described as a gaping maw compressing, chewing it to digest somewhere deep in its belly, deep underground… below their very feet.

Sarah stared at the net wondering how long the disc had been inside. She could make out the corner of it, thin and yellow underneath the moss and dirt, buried beneath the skeleton of something tiny, something indecipherable on quick glance, but obviously mammal if you dared to stare. It was the disc you used for long distances, the one that could land you within dunking range if you could throw it straight. It had the number 17 scratched on the bottom.

Grace found herself on a bridge staring at the wreckage beneath it: an engine, a rudder, a refrigerator door.

Vials… full, empty, pretty, red.

There were holes in the bridge.

There were holes.

Red, red, everything red.

Pulsing.

Swaying.

Writhing in the wind, dancing to an unheard melody.

Lori started to say something to them all but didn't. She didn't need to. It reached up from the car, out of the cab of the truck, though the netting, up between the slats to caress their faces as red seeds somersaulted in the wind.

# IN SERVICE OF HER

IT HURTS MORE than she says it will. Especially when she needs.

She's not gentle when she is blinded by want. Nothing she does can trick me into thinking it will be ok, that I'll enjoy it too, even though she tries.

It's the pulling that hurts the worst.

The piercing, the skin giving way to the intruder, the digging for purchase—none of that is as bad as the first pull, the first suck, that coax to get the blood flowing. My muscles fight against it. My very veins draw away, shrinking from it in fear even as my mind bids me stay still. Fighting it is futile. Fighting it only makes it worse.

She doesn't mean to hurt me, but the syringe was a bother. And anyway there was something about the sinking of the teeth into my skin that sent a tingle down her spine, made her sigh. No, she didn't mean to hurt me. Doing so would only hurt her more in the long run. Who would pay the bills, keep the house, keep up appearances? Who would hunt for her, lure the pretty, make them feel like they were important, smart, needed all so that she could have them when she wanted them? Sure, she could find another, someone else to play the familiar and do whatever she wants, but would she find one so willing to bare their neck when she wanted it, to mount on demand and be mounted if commanded? Would she find someone to endure the pain, the vice-like grip that everything that looked beautiful on her offered, the cruel duality of her essence threatening to rip him to shreds? Many would die under such weight. Many would rather kill themselves than endure it more than once. But I am trained. I know when to bark and when to heel.

There's never much to clean up when all is said and done.

And that was good.

And sometimes she smiles on me when she's done, sapphires in pinky rings and thick links of gold mine for the keeping, like the leash around my neck.

# I SEE

I SEE blue skies with cotton ball clouds hanging over my head ready to dump the rain they carry onto me.

I see pineapples on the vine
Pumpkins roots crawling, spreading,
invading
permeating
dominating
waiting.

Blood oranges pinpricked, crying thick, sappy tears for me to see.

And
I
see flowers with hair for petals,
eyes that roll in sockets too weak to hold them still.

Flies land on the lidless things, bite at the flesh, dip their feet in the carnage, let it soak in deep, and then rub them together.

I see want on her lips,
blood red and foul,
smelling of waste and false promises.

Wipe it away
Smear it like so much lipstick drawing on pale cheeks.
A crayon on canvas.
Lick the juice from the pocked skin, bitter and sweet to
trick the senses
Bittersweet like wool on a summer's day
to trick the mob
to fool the fool.
I see orange light under a black sky and bite my lip
make it bleed
to pay for passage.

# THE NEIGHBORS

THE SUN WAS HOT.

She spiraled her wrist, jostling the ice in her drink, ice that was melting rapidly, watering down what was left of her Arnold Palmer. The ice clinked against the side of the glass, and it was rhythmic; it was mesmerizing, and she wondered about the things that lived between the spaces of each chime.

*Clink*

Why was her drink called an Arnold Palmer? Just because some golf guy liked a little sweet with his sour didn't mean he should get a drink named after him-

*Clink*

Why was it so damned hot? It felt like the sun had moved closer to the world, closer to her town, settling right over her house to heat the air, warm her skin, melt her ice—

*Clink*

What time was it? It was already past noon—she knew that much—so why was it as hot as hell itself in the middle of the afternoon? No, it wasn't even afternoon anymore—it was evening... right? She had finished making tuna pasta salad, had put it in the fridge right before coming out to read. That was at least an hour ago—

*Clink*

When does evening start? Like, technically? 5 pm… 6? Doesn't the sun have to be setting for it to really be evening? Can you even call it evening if it isn't actually getting dark? What if the sun never rises to be able to set later in the day, like in some part of Alaska during winter?

*Clink*

Is it Alaska? Where the sun doesn't rise… Alaska, right? Wait maybe that's where the *midnight* sun happens—where it never *sets*—not the other way around. Either way, God! How do they live like that? How can they stand it being light all the time?

*Clink*

*'The midnight sun will never set… it shines forever in my heart…'* Who sang that? Billie Holiday? No, her voice wasn't as introspective as Billie's. Dinah Washington? Carmen McRae? No—deeper, haunting. How could I forget! The Divine One. Sarah Vaughan-

*Clink*

Condensation wet her fingers as her mind twisted and turned, whiling the day away.

The trees whispered answers to her unspoken questions, helping her piece together the puzzles her mind occupied itself with.

*Shhhhh*

*Clink*

*Shhhhh*

*Clink*

The hair at her temples was damp, sticking to her skin in dark swaths. Dark *yellow* swaths. She knew what they looked like without having to check; she had already caught a glimpse of how wrong the color was in the shower that morning. Near perfect when dry, golden with chestnut high-lights and glossy—so very glossy—but when it was wet it was the most ridiculous shade ever. Artificial. Deliberate. Fake. She felt like everyone could see the partitioning, could see where the highlight foil added visual interest. When it was wet the whole damned thing looked like it came out of a box. And even though it did, that was beside the point. It was a damned expensive box, if that's what it came down to, and if Everett wanted her to continue paying for it, he'd better fix this—

*Slam*

A new sound.

Broke up the ice and tree duet.

Made her jump.

Her Arnold Palmer shot up like a geyser, almost came out of the glass onto her hand.

It was loud—louder than it should have been.

Her neighbor.

Thirty feet between the houses yet the sound was loud enough to rip her away from her thoughts. Now she felt like she could hear everything, every creak of the wood planks on the deck, the whine the chairs made as whoever had come outside laid something upon them. Who was it—Jeff? Or was his name John?

Or… Jack?

Jerry?

Wait… was it Pat?

Mike?

Rick?

Shit.

She had never taken the time to learn their names, commit them to memory. How long had it been—three years since they moved in? They had bought the place after Jason and Kim moved to New York, some new opportunity opening up for her that, for some reason, couldn't be done remotely. She didn't know if she believed that—*everything* was online now. You could have doctor consultations online, order groceries.. You could even do house walk-thrus online now, which is exactly what Jason and Kim had done. There might have been a job opportunity, but it was more likely that they were sick of it all. Tired of the grass, tired of the HOA, tired of having to drive 20 minutes to go shopping, no access to anything but the family movie theater and mom and pop restaurants.

Sick of the sticks.

She sniffed, remembered a conversation in their kitchen a few years back. Jason had said that they were living in suburban hell without the benefits. And yeah, it was true—sometimes she could feel the cows closing in on their little development, the cement sidewalks, identical mailboxes, and paved trails encircling the complex not enough to keep rurality at bay. But for her, the sound of the wind working its way through the leaves beat police sirens and elevated voices any day.

They left, and those people came, and she hadn't been in the house since. Not that she had been over there a lot when Jason and Kim lived there—Jason worked from home and was always on one call or another and Kim... well, she was Kim. But still they had gone over a few times and had the couple over to their house a time or two also, but now Jessica or Jennifer or whatever her name was wasn't letting them in.

Her eyebrow arched reflexively.

Maybe that was a stretch.

Whatever.

The bottom line was that there had been no invitation for drinks or game night. No afternoon chats or sharing a grocery run.

Jeff/Jack/Pat/Mike raised a hand and smiled, all teeth and charm above his tie dye t-shirt.

And that was that.

Who didn't call over to their neighbor and comment on the weather?

Who didn't ask how they've been, offer them a drink, chitchat about garbage pickup or the mailman leaving the mailbox door open or people letting their dogs defecate on their lawn and not picking it up?

All of the other people on the street did… at least the ones on their street. They greeted each other as they walked by, talked while standing on their respective driveways, kids and dogs running circles around their legs. They stopped mowing their lawns to talk about gas prices or the new recycling pick up schedule. They were fucking neighborly.

*She* was neighborly.

But maybe they weren't like that where they were from.

He was sorting things out on the grill station—from where she sat it looked like seasonings and sauce, maybe some bread or buns. Maybe it was a rub for ribs? She couldn't really tell. She peered closer, dropping her foot from the chair it was propped up on so that she could lean forward lower, closer, nearer.

Not ribs.

Some kind of meat, but not ribs.

She could only see the pink flesh through the new fancy black aluminum balusters they installed. Damned thing looked like a gate. What had been so wrong with the deck railings that were there before? Jason and Kim had had the deck inspected before they put it up for sale, and they were just fine. But no, Jeff/Jack/Pat/Mike and Jessica/Jennifer needed something *different*… something *special*. Just had to waste money on a fancy cedar deck with black rails on the back of their house where nobody would ever see. A fancy deck that looked like a gate. Like bars at a jail. What were they trying to keep in? What were they trying to hide?

"Almost too hot to grill," he said, and she almost didn't hear him. She was fully leaned over by then; the angle of her body was so severe, she was nearly coming out of her seat. Could he see her? Maybe. But maybe not. She had heard he didn't see well from a distance.

She sat up gradually anyway, hoping her movement wouldn't be noticed.

"Y-yes," she stammered as she fought the urge to pat at her hair and smooth her skirt. That was something her mother would have done, her hands always fluttering in an effort to tidy when she got nervous. When had she become like her, patting, fidgeting, fiddling under the weight of a man's stare? She didn't know, and she wouldn't let herself wonder about it too long because to do so would turn her attention to the real question hanging in the air.

He smiled and turned back to his hunk of meat, big and marbled with fat.

Did he smile... or did he smirk?

She was afraid to keep looking and find out.

He was fiddling with the meat—she could almost hear the squelching of the juices as he massaged it smugly, so smugly like he owned the place, could almost smell the seasonings he rubbed into the flesh, the arrogant bastard, could almost smell the blood...

The wife or girlfriend—she didn't even know if they were married—told her that they were from just outside Washington, DC, when they were moving in. The movers had had to work hard that day—there were so many boxes to unload, such many heavy wood pieces to bring in. But there were a few boxes that they wouldn't let anyone touch. A few that only Jessica/Jennifer and Jeff/Jack/Pat/Mike touched. What was in there?

Unmentionables?

She couldn't help but laugh at herself. Unmentionables... what even *was* that? And how old was she all of a sudden? Had sitting out in the sun cooked her brain? There had to be a better word for girly magazines and toys than that, even if it had been a while since she had thought about those kinds of things...

No, that's not the point. What she and William did or didn't do in the bedroom was not the point at all, although some nights, when she was awake and the snoring beside her drove her mad, forced her up and out of the bed, out of the room... sometimes she wondered what the sounds she heard carried on the wind were, sounds that could have been born of pleasure as easily as of agony, sounds that seemed like they were right next to her.

They had a dog.

The day they moved in there was a dog on a leash being led by a little boy. He looked like he might have only been nine years old—the girl, presumably his sister, was a little bit older. The dog was just a baby, a pup of around 4 months by the looks of it. A mutt. A shaggy little thing who would grow into his paws before they knew it and then eat them out of house and home. Like the boy would.

The boy and the puppy would start eating, and eating, and eating, consuming everything they could get their hands on. And it would be so much, too much to keep up with, everything Jessica/Jennifer and Jeff/Jack/Pat/Mike bought would be eaten, sucked in, swallowed whole.

She hadn't seen the dog in a long time.

The boy was two inches taller now than he had been that day.

Was Jeff/Jack/Pat/Mike smiling or was he smirking as he finished massaging the meat and opened the grill lid, effectively blocking her view of him, his house, and everything he wanted to keep secret? Because that's what it was, wasn't it? He was keeping secrets. People like that, ones that keep to themselves, don't invite their neighbors inside, and set their grills up so that they block the world out when they cook – those people are always keeping secrets... aren't they? Hiding behind something like they hide behind the grill lid. But hiding from what? Keeping secrets about what, she wondered? And why? The prospect gave her chills. Were they running from something they did back wherever they came from? They moved in fast after the sale—was that why? Did they take something with them when they left, bring it here, hide it somewhere in the house? Is that why they never invited her over—because she might see—

"I can't believe you're still out here, Mom."

She hadn't noticed the door opening and closing nor her daughter coming out onto the deck, but there she was, dressed in a white sundress that showed off her curves. She remembered when she used to look like that in a dress, remembered when she would let the sun kiss the tops of her shoulders, smiled when it left tan lines there to remember it by. It wasn't that she couldn't wear a sundress now—she could... she exercised four times a week, didn't smoke, didn't drink... much. But it was different now—gravity had had its way, and what a bitch she had been about things.

"What time is it?" she said, sounding as if she were coming out of a fog.

"Almost dinnertime."

She nodded. William had talked about shish kebob. She wondered if he needed help.

"I brought you another drink. I figured yours had to be watered down by now," Krista said cheerfully.

She loved the sound of her daughter's voice. So melodic, so lyrical. She was cavalier, worry-free, stressless, and you could tell. Her voice was airy and light, confident and nonplussed. Like a bird chirping in the sky. She marveled at the thought of her pretty girl with her pretty boyfriend and her pretty life.

She looked into her glass and smiled. She rubbed her hand over her daughter's cheek in thanks.

"Oh look, it's like yours!"

Another Arnold Palmer. Her favorite. A few ice cubes and a wedge of lemon to top it off. And this time William had frozen the cubes fast enough. The iris was still hazel.

# BLIP

---

"WHAT THE HELL?"

Laurie couldn't stop herself from saying it, even though she'd been trying not to curse as much since life had changed and the kids were now at home during the day. But it was hard, harder than it should have been—harder than she would ever admit out loud that it was. Oh, who was she fooling? Everybody in the house knew she was having a hard time keeping her language PC. Some days she gave up trying before lunch. But this time she had been in the middle of a report, and yes, she had saved it, but not in the past five minutes, and she had been on a roll typing, cutting and pasting, damnit, she was almost finished. So, yeah, she cursed out loud. 'Hell' wasn't as bad as what she almost let slip.

"Nooooooo!" was the call from downstairs from a voice that sounded a lot deeper now than it had when the pandemic started, a voice that was attached to a kid who was also taller than he had been before the world went to hell in handbasket—a kid who was taller than her now. That wasn't saying much with her being all of 5'4", but still. Seven months ago she was looking him in the eye, and now she most definitely was not.

The other one didn't say anything—probably didn't even notice anything because she was on her phone. It seemed like overnight the phone had fused with her hand like an appendage, and even though she couldn't make calls on it yet, she could do everything else: learn makeup tips from people who painted their faces to look like cheetahs and then somehow made it all come together into something beautiful, listen to songs that teetered on the edge of questionable, the lyrics clipped just before parents' ears would perk up and pay attention, fawn over some boy band from another country and learn words that nobody else in the house understood. Thank you, COVID-19, for the premature teenaging.

The hum of the house kicked back on not even three seconds after it turned off, adding insult to injury because she knew it was too damned late to salvage anything. Because Laurie wasn't using her laptop, not right then—she was signed into a meeting on her laptop, but the report she was writing was being created on her desktop. Why? Because she was a dinosaur, that's why, and she was kicking herself for it now. The laptop hummed along during the power surge, only offering a slight hesitation when the power cut off—just enough to miss a word or two from the fast-talking New Yorker who didn't know the answer to the question he had been asked but was trying to talk himself toward some kind of solution anyway. The laptop, thanks to its nifty battery pack, stayed on while her desktop summarily cut off, no fade to black for good ole' Betsy, no, just now you see it, now you don't. When the power came back Betsy waited for Laurie to boot her back up, the old bitch, and Laurie obliged, knowing what she would find—the saved copy of the work she had completed before her coffee break, all formatted and spellchecked to boot—ooh, she could be so anal about things sometimes—but the work she had completed in the past few minutes were gone with the wind.

Laurie remembered when she and Rob had talked about homeschooling—remembered how she was dead set against it. And there were so many reasons to be against it, she thought as she listened to the CPU booting up again, hoping the power stayed on long enough for her to email the document she had been working on to her work email so she could finish it on her laptop, but she had her doubts. There were at least seven other households filled to the gills on her street alone thanks to the pandemic, and that was nothing compared to what it would look like when everybody had to give up the ghost and stay home. They had to vie for connectivity and power all day, things that were usually in abundant supply. When the world was normal, there were only maybe 35 people working from home in their 400-house community. But now, with just about half of her community (which ended up being more representative of her county and even her state than she ever expected) having their kids go to school online at home, there were more people than she could identify by face toiling around in their houses. Sometimes she looked out of her window and saw people taking walks, which was normal under any circumstances, but these were people she had never laid eyes on before. People she had never seen in the supermarket, in the restaurants on what they called restaurant row, the cleaners. Not even in Target, and it seemed like everybody she knew or knew of in her little town ended up in Target at least once a week. When the pandemic hit and people started to work from home or lost their jobs or whatever happened to them, there were people milling about that she hadn't even known existed.

The Punjabi family.

The couple speaking what she thought might have been Dutch and walking at a fast clip no doubt racking up steps on their Fitbits.

The Nigerian grandmother who taught her how to say 'I love you' in Yoruba after Laurie heard her yelling, "Mo ni ife re!" to her children as they drove away (that was before things got too bad. Laurie couldn't help but wonder if she has seen them since, thinks she should maybe check in on the woman to see if she needed anything).

Laurie was also getting used to people's habits—like the guy who drank coffee on his front porch in his bathrobe, come rain or shine, and the kid who rode his bike down the middle of the road, always popping a wheelie where it curved.

Every. Single. Day.

She had even stopped being startled by the family—all five of them… mom, dad, daughter, and two sons, each under the age of 10—who took their daily walk at 2:30 in the morning. Laurie had to believe there was a reason for it being so late—maybe the dad worked the nightshift or the mom worked overnight in one of the big box stores. It couldn't be that they were a bunch of vampires, looking for somebody's blood to suck… right…?

They weren't… hunting for meat yet, were they?

It couldn't have come down to that already… right?

No, of course not. The bigger question, and she had to remind herself about this often enough, was why she was up to see them on their daily jaunt in the first place?

Dogs barked.

Cars passed by.

All seemingly on cue.

Sometimes she felt like whipping her head around fast to try and catch the camera crew recording her life like she was the new Truman in The Truman Show: Pandemic Style. That would be strange, but so was staying six feet away from everybody and wearing masks every time you stepped outside. So was looking up recipes to make hand sanitizer because you can't find any in the stores.

*Blip.*

Careful Miss, your slip is showing.

Booting up slowly, but booting up.

The boy still yelling downstairs, so close to dropping a curse of his own, she thinks she almost hears it, wonders distantly if she'll say anything about it if it does fall out of his mouth, or if she'll let it slide this time. Rob was lucky he missed all of this stuff, if you could call that lucky. He was usually stuck at work, the firefighters sleeping in on the job bunking together like they were in dorms. When she was feeling sentimental she thought he might actually miss them, miss their little family and all the noise that came with it. But then she imagined booze, and ashtrays overflowing with butts, tables filled with take-out wrappers, videogames, and porn playing on the big screen, and she realized how silly she had been.

Kid stomping up the stairs.

The man-child coming.

Taller, taller. Laurie had time to think that if her daughter, curiously silent but almost looking her right in the eye at age 11, kept growing at the rate she currently was, she'd be taller than Laurie in a year or so before her son started in.

"It's so messed up!" he said, pacing in front of her, the sound he made against the floor too loud for what she envisioned coming from his six-year-old feet. "I was in the middle of a match!"

"It was a power surg-"

"I know, Mom, but I was in the middle of a match! We couldn't get on all day—somebody always had something else to do—and now, when we *finally* get in, this happens."

147

*Oh, God, what will we do if we miss the match?!*

*It's been ALL DAY LONG*, even though all day amounts to maybe two hours now, at noon.

*My life will be over if I can't get into this match, you don't understand, for real, no cap, honest, on the real, yo, you just don't get it, man.*

A smile crept onto Laurie's lips as she considered the back and forth that could happen if she responded the wrong way. It was comical, really, how worked up he could get over matches and arsenals and power packs and whatever else went on in the world of the game he and his friends connected in. And she supposed that was ok. Because stuck in the house like they were, that world was his world, at least for right now. And in that world he could run around outside and jump off stuff and break down doors and dance over people when he did it. Just like in her daughter's world she could learn dances and post them and get likes and thank people for them and then do it all over again.

"Jes—" Laurie started, but the man-child cut her off again with more of his ranting.

"—Dave is like never on—"

*Probably because his parents find other things for him to do. They are better parents than me, I guess.*

She shook her head and knew he didn't understand why, and that was ok.

It was still quiet upstairs.

But not where Laurie was. No, not at all.

"—planned since yesterday," Bobby continued, "and now it's all messed u—."

"Jessie?" Laurie yelled up the stairs like she did so often, letting her voice carry rather than climbing them.

Her son kept talking, undeterred. He was flapping his arms, nearly flinging himself around the foyer.

Laurie thought the stench that every parent stuck in the

house with kids aged 10 and over knew all too well might knock her out.

No answer.

"Jess—Bobby, hang on a second, ok?"

Teeth sucking.

Sighing.

Laurie almost laughed.

"Jessie, honey?"

… what? Are you ok? That's what Laurie wanted to ask for some reason, but why? What could be wrong? Jessie was upstairs looking at her phone like usual and from where she was, likely on her bed propped up on that furry armchair pillow thing on her bed that's on its last legs, nothing had even happened. If she had her earbuds in, Jessie hadn't even heard Laurie call her name.

Technology… gotta love it.

"Mom!" Bobby groaned, and for some reason Laurie was accosted with the memory of his father catching his toe on something as they waded into the water in, where was that, Aruba? Barbados? She couldn't remember. She had been waiting for him to get in the water—he took his sweet time putting on sunscreen and putting his hat and sunglasses somewhere safe so they wouldn't fly away, get up and walk away—whatever it was he was afraid of. Everything he was doing was so slow and methodical. Laurie thought she was going to jump out of her skin. She wanted to get in the water, to feel the sand between her toes, to taste the saltiness of it on her lips. And when they finally waded in, when the vacation finally started to feel real, Laurie heard Rob scream. Laurie didn't remember if it sounded exactly the same as Bobby did as he called out to her in complete and total frustration, but it might as well have. And from underwater on some sunny day in her past, how was she to know that she would hear that sound again, somewhere down the line from the kid who calls the screamer 'dad', his namesake, as melo-dramatic as he was. She dove underwater that day, acting like she didn't hear him, buying herself maybe a minute more of bliss. She wished there were something to duck under right then.

"What if I can't get back in—?"

"Go check," Laurie said, before looking at her computer to make sure they had connectivity and that he could actually log in. She just wanted him out of there, wanted to stop the onslaught of his yelling and the funk of not washing in days because nobody was going anywhere, wanted to silence the grating pitch his voice was taking on. And that was ok. She wasn't up for the Mother of the Year award anyway, not this year, "but go check on Jessie first," she heard herself saying.

Laurie hadn't looked away from the door, hadn't realized she was planning to send her first up to see about her second, but she had done it, and now it was out there. Bobby sighed again and mumbled something under his breath but started toward the stairs anyway, calling Jessie's name once more, hoping she'd save him the trip. When he settled down enough to notice, Bobby could see that there was something about the way Laurie was staring up at the stairs from behind her desk, hardly moving a muscle, that didn't allow any room for questions.

If Laurie had ever had the chance to tell the story, she would have said that Bobby, her sweet boy who looked like her uncle more and more every day with his hair growing long in the quarantine, but not unpleasantly so, only made it up one stair before it happened. She would have said that they were both taken aback because he had been in the base-ment and she had been on the main floor and Jessie most certainly had not been on either of those. She would have had to have been to be where she was right then but she hadn't been—they were sure of it. But there she was, outside, looking at them through the window, the blinds open just enough to let in some light but closed enough to keep out some of the heat that sometimes came on fall afternoons, those days when Laurie found herself dressing and redressing, trying to keep up with weather that was inherently schizophrenic during that time of year. There she was, outside the house with no way of getting there, unless she had climbed out of her window and jumped down. But she couldn't have done that either, not and just walked away from it. And besides, the alarm hadn't gone off when Jessie opened the window... *if* she had opened the window... which she couldn't have... Laurie was sure about that too.

Jessie was smiling.

A dog was walking.

The powerwalking elderly couple were pumping their arms, their neon orange weights glowing as they went about their normal routine.

Bobby was on the stairs.

Jessie was smiling, but there were too many teeth. Too many in her preteen mouth, too many for an adult's.

Something wet was dripping, pooling somewhere on a carpet; the wet, plopping sound was deafening.

There was a whine, something faint, almost not there. Like a sound caught in the back of someone's throat when the thing they were most afraid of looked like it might really be coming for them, like a dog who knew it was trapped and begs for mercy because it ought to, but knows it won't get it.

Like the sound of the electricity going out everywhere, for the last time.

Lips working, undulating, pulling back to reveal bloody gums, puckering out in a grotesque kiss and through it all, she was smiling, her lips splitting, gore spilling out, all mucus and puss tinged with red.

The lights flickered.

The power turned off again.

*One*

*Two*

*Three*

"Ghaawwwwdddd, *what?*" Jessie yelled and flung open her bedroom door to find her brother standing in a pool of urine and her mother's mouth open so wide it was if her jaw had distended, unhinged, broken. They were staring at the window, staring so intensely that they hadn't heard her... until they weren't.

Laurie and Bobby whipped their heads toward Jessie so fast, Bobby lost his balance and fell against the wall. She would have laughed were it not for the looks on their faces. Surprise—like really, she scared the hell out of Bobby and deep down, she was happy about that. At least he actually *saw* her for once—ever since they had been locked away in their house, Bobby had only noticed her if she was standing in front of the TV. But it was more than just surprise. There was also confusion on their faces, like they didn't understand what they were looking at. And something else, though it took her brain a few cycles to get to it—fear.

They were afraid.

Black lines in front of her eyes, encasing Bobby and her mother too. Black lines like borders on a picture, like bars on a jail cell. Shimmering, waving, moving, like hot meeting cold on an abandoned blacktop

*Four*

and it was getting darker around them, darker around her mother, blurring her face behind it, creeping into her open mouth. Jessie called to them, but they didn't hear her. She reached out, but her hand met the black bars instead, and they felt solid even as her hand dove into them as if they were water, sank in there and tingled in the unseen space.

The cellphone in her other hand was warm, so warm, too warm.

Her hand was in the bars, disappeared at the wrist and prickling like it had fallen asleep... like a thousand needles were bouncing off of it—not penetrating, but bouncing, bouncing, bouncing like her hand was a trampoline and the needles were who had been stuck inside the house for too long.

Jessie yanked her hand back, and it wouldn't come, it wouldn't come, and she screamed for her momma and her brother and they didn't hea—

*Blip.*

Made in the USA
Columbia, SC
21 September 2024

42095013R00095